CHASE HUGHES

THE BELGRADE ARCHER

Book 2

PIERCE RESTON SERIES

The Belgrade Archer

ISBN: ISBN: 978-1-7351416-1-9

RDP83-01074R000200150001-2

Published by Evergreen Press
Milton, DE

WARNING:

This book contains fictional depictions of hypnotic-coded language, which can cause a listener, and in some cases, a reader to become entranced or suggestible. Do not operate any heavy machinery or include yourself in dangerous or potentially dangerous activities while experiencing *The Belgrade Archer.*

For Michelle

True power resides not in our leaders, but in those who keep their secrets.

"I, Pierce Reston, do hereby and hereon offer my life in defense of peace. As a member of HIG, I pledge, promise, and duly swear to hold the peace of humanity higher than any law of the land. On this day, my graduation, I make a solemn vow, as many have before me, to preserve by any and all means, the secrets to which I have been entrusted.

I fully encumber this burden in the name of peace. I will live above the common level of life and act as a role model, even in the absence of a witness.

The secrets that have been passed on to me are sacred. I will forever protect them, and am prepared to do so with my life. I will never cause these secrets to be exposed except in circumstances that warrant their use.

On this day I assume the full and arduous burden of my fellow man. On this day, my life is no longer my own; it belongs to the peace of our family on Earth."

CHAPTER 1

Norfolk, Virginia

It shot into his ears, up his spine, and jolted his entire body.

The security alert siren Captain Cooper had hoped never to hear screamed through his office, violently replacing the hum of the air system in his stateroom. Yelling erupted from the ship's corridors only seconds later.

Chief Gibbs thrust his head into the doorway. "There's something weird in the water down here, Captain."

Cooper struggled to hear the man's words over the rhythmic drone of the alarm. "In the water? We're tied to the pier!" he shouted through the noise, his body instinctively already out of his chair.

He stabbed his feet back into his workout shoes and followed closely behind the chief where two men stood watch in dress uniform.

"What's going on?" he shouted. The security alarm blared through the salty morning air, bouncing off the nearby ships in the harbor.

The rising sun glared off rain puddles on the wide concrete piers. On what would have been a quiet morning, the jarring alarm forced hundreds of potential disaster scenarios through his mind like endless scrolling television channels, each with their own catastrophe playing out.

The chief shook his head. "Sir, there's something in the water here—looks like a big ol' boat turned upside down." The man's usually tanned face was almost silver and slack with panic. "Sir, it...has antennas coming out of it. Big ones."

Without a word, Cooper spun and raced up the steep series of stairs to the ship's command tower. He rounded the corner, stepped up to the lookout platform and swiveled the heavy, mounted binoculars toward the floating object, only a hundred yards from the Aircraft Carrier in the next dock over.

He paused, letting his eyes adjust. It *did* look like a huge, upturned boat, but it definitely wasn't. Four towering antennas shot skyward from the object's forward surface. He leveled the binoculars on the front of the object and his breathing stopped. Blood drained from his face. Below the surface, in the darkness, a long, black form took shape. His heartbeat hammered in his ears.

"Jesus Christ."

He swallowed hard, recoiled away from the binoculars, and blinked to refocus. He pressed his eyes to the binoculars and saw it just below the surface: a faded yellow Russian Navy emblem.

Not an upturned boat.

He stared in frozen disbelief at the lifeless Russian Nuclear Submarine, adrift in the harbor. The sharp spring breeze whipped strings of sea spray across its mammoth surface.

Cooper leapt from the platform and shot into the bridge. He snatched the emergency red phone handset and squeezed the talk button; his hand shook.

"All ships. All ships. All ships. This is X-Ray Seven. Emergency security alert. Enemy Russian submarine in the harbor at Pier Fifteen. Recommend secure all hatches for potential explosion or attack, over."

Within seconds, the security alarms of the other ships echoed through the harbor, the sound echoing off every nearby structure in chaotic chimes. Sailors on nearby ships scrambled—equally shocked at the unfolding chaos.

Cooper ran back to the binoculars and leveled them again on the submarine. The uppermost hatch was laid open. Dead quiet. The giant, lifeless machine swayed, at the mercy of the wind. He stepped back from the binoculars and covered his mouth.

Whatever happens today, a war has begun.

CHAPTER 2

Yorktown, Virginia

Pierce Reston threw the cool sheets to the side and rolled toward the bedside table. A green 6:04 AM flashed on the ancient alarm clock he'd had since childhood. A clack echoed in the room and Pierce instinctively reached for the grip of his Glock under the adjacent pillow. It was gone.

The door to his right inched open. Pierce's breath caught in his throat.

A woman with flawless skin, wearing nothing but a bathrobe, emerged from the doorway holding two cups of coffee. Her dark, shoulder-length hair sprang outward in unkempt protest.

Pierce's muscles relaxed—a long breath escaped.

"You okay?" Kelly tilted her head.

"Yeah. Sorry. Not used to humans being here."

Kelly smiled and placed a hot cup of coffee on Pierce's nightstand. "I'm jumping in the shower. You've got missed calls from Deidra."

Pierce, in his underwear, threw a grey t-shirt on. He trudged his way into the kitchen and pulled the cable from his phone.

Two missed calls

He tapped on the notification and the phone rang twice.

"Pierce?" Her voice shook; raw and unmasked.

"Yes, ma'am. We're—I'm awake. What's up?" He wiped his eyes, blinking the bleariness from them.

"There's a Russian submarine in Norfolk harbor. It's empty. The crew is gone."

A wave of heat pounded into his stomach.

"Pierce?"

"Yes. Yes, ma'am. I'll be right in. Please send whatever you can to my iPad and I'll read-in before I get there."

"It's all on your iPad now. I've sent the news briefings as well. The media is going crazy, Pierce. I need you in here, quick."

Pierce darted into the bathroom where Kelly stood before the mirror drying her hair. She met Pierce's gaze. "I've already been recalled to HIG. You too?"

Pierce nodded. "Let's take separate cars. I don't want anyone—"

Kelly spun the hairdryer around and sent a wave of hot air into Pierce's face before lowering it with a grin. "I know. Me either."

Pierce hauled on a clean pair of jeans and a grey polo shirt. As he slid his feet into a pair of boat shoes, he tapped out a message to Deidra.

> *Need a prep-call to the Naval base in Norfolk. Let them know there's a high-level State Department official coming down. I'll need as much access as I can get.*

"I'll see you at HIG," Pierce yelled through the doorway.

"Got it! See you there!"

Pierce hefted his go-bag over his shoulder, scraped his car keys off the kitchen counter, and climbed into his antique Jaguar, bound for HIG. The car speakers came to life in the middle of a breaking news announcement. ". . . and the naval base went into a full lockdown, and traffic bound for Naval Station Norfolk is at a complete standstill right now. Russian Prime Minister Andrei Petrov has issued a public statement that the US has illegally captured the submarine and is likely holding the crew hostage," a woman said.

A deep male voice came through immediately afterward. "I can't imagine the conspiracy theories being spun up right now. This thing apparently floats to the surface only a few yards from one of our aircraft carriers. Initial reports are saying the submarine was discovered this morning. To me, that's scary; I mean, how was this thing not detected by our military? If Russia wants a fight because they lost a submarine, then let's show them—"

Pierce slapped the power button.

Idiots.

If there was anything these people were excellent at, it was making fear contagious. In his younger days at HIG, Alex had uttered a phrase Pierce would never forget. "Fear is the most certain way to increase predictability in human beings."

As he pulled into the gravel driveway of HIG, an unfamiliar scene emerged; under the covered drive, a grey tent stood over a row of clunky black computers and printers. Four men in full tactical gear stood at the ready beside a black armored transport van that HIG hadn't used in years.

Once inside, Pierce froze in the kitchen. Amidst the quiet hum of refrigerators, an oil painting had locked him in place. Wrapped in a golden, elegant frame, the painting of a man wearing a dark suit hung on the stone wall. He still had not adjusted to seeing it. The weather-worn face of his friend and mentor, Alex Frost, stared back with a timeless gaze of composure and maturity. Pierce's chin tightened at the memory of his death. He missed the way Alex had always shown him that even the most complex problems have simple solutions.

He vividly recalled the day Alex had recruited him to join HIG. The moment he was introduced to the capabilities of Tradecraft.

Only twelve years prior, Alex Frost had changed his life in one solitary five-minute conversation . . .

He had trained where all CIA officers learned espionage: The Farm, a base hidden deep within Camp Peary, Virginia. One evening after training at the schoolhouse, Pierce sat drinking alone at a local favorite of soon-to-be agents, The Green Leafe Café. He quietly reviewed notes from the day's training in espionage tradecraft amidst clinking plates and conversations. His attention shifted when a stranger settled into the seat across from him as if they were long-acquainted friends meeting for a beer. Pierce didn't miss the way the older man's eyes flicked around the room, taking a quick assessment of his surroundings—definitely not a civilian.

The man not-so-subtly slipped Pierce's waiter a hundred-dollar bill and, with a grin on his tranquil, timeworn face, said, "It's on me; keep the change." His tanned skin and sharp outfit had jumped straight from the pages of a Ralph Lauren ad. As he lowered himself into his seat, his polo shirt offered no hint of a concealed weapon, and he kept his leathery hands flat on the table.

Pierce narrowed his eyes, silent. He clocked the Rolex on the man's wrist and noted the man's left hand was several shades lighter than his right.

Golf-glove tan. Right-handed. Has money. No weapon. Big government, maybe.

The aged man leaned against the table and spoke to Pierce in a smooth, hushed voice. "You've got nothing to worry about." He raised his palms in submission. "I've just come here to offer my thanks for your service to our country and ask you a question."

His deep, calm voice carried the heft of an old-time radio host. Pierce relaxed the grip on his knife under the table; the man was obviously not here to kill him. He feigned confusion, pulling his eyebrows together. "Service to the country?"

The stranger shook his head. "You don't have to say a word about that. Just wanted to say thanks." His weathered hand slid a crisp, black, American diplomatic passport across the table.

"Look, man, I have no interest in seeing your ID, or even—"

"It's not my ID, son. It's yours," he interrupted.

Pierce glanced around the bar, searching for signs someone else was involved with this man. Nothing. He lifted the thick cover of the document with the back of his finger, making minimal contact with it. A photo of himself stared up from the passport. Beside his picture was the name Timothy Martien.

Pierce eyed his full glass of beer sweating into the napkin on the table and met the man's stare. "You know that last name means Martian in French, right? Like, a person from Mars?"

The older man chuckled loudly and leaned back in his seat. His unwavering, fatherly gaze was disarming, but Pierce had endured countless tests of his integrity at the CIA. Every conversation could turn out to be something vastly different than it seemed.

Pierce relaxed. A moment passed. He took a few deep breaths. The man broke the silence.

"I can assure you, Mister Reston, that this is no test."

He knew his name. Pierce fought a searing curiosity to find out how.

"I don't work for 'The Company,'" the man continued. "I'd like to offer you a new job. Would you allow me to prove it to you? If not, I'll leave immediately, and you'll never see me again."

Pierce slid his notebook to the side. "I'm all ears, Mister..."

"Frost. Alex Frost. *Real name*. I can assure you I'm not working for any foreign government, Mister Reston. If I wanted to turn you against your country, it would take me all of about four minutes to do so."

The bustle of the bar swelled around them. Pierce chortled. He leaned back into the wooden bench seat and lifted his beer glass off the table. It rose much more easily than expected. Pierce eyed it in disbelief. Half the beer had vanished.

The old man, Frost, leaned in again and lowered his voice. "Pierce—may I call you Pierce?"

"S-sure. Yeah."

"Pierce, I've been watching your progress for a while. I'd like to show you what we do, and I'd like you to work for us. Think of one thing no one else on earth would ever know. Something that not even your diary, a therapist, or even friends and family would know. Just think about it; you don't have to say a word."

Pierce mused at the idea. There was one thing he had kept sacred since he was nine years old. He and a friend had watched *Red Dawn*, a movie about a Russian invasion of the United States. He and his friend had set up a secret series of four, two-word passcodes over their walkie talkies to ensure it was really them on the other end of the radio—the Russians in the movie could speak English, so Pierce and his friend invented words of their own. He would say the first secret phrase, and his friend would reply with the second, and so on. It was juvenile, but he'd never forgotten the ultra-secret series of made-up words.

"Are you thinking of it now?" Frost asked.

Pierce shot a bemused smile at the man and nodded as he took a sip of cold beer.

Alex leaned in and whispered, "Adi Skoff. Raadi Haas. Ringo Stuture. Lamvo Saadi."

Pierce stiffened. He jerked forward and plunked the beer on the table. "Who the hell—?"

Alex Frost held up a hand with a paternal, empathetic smile. "*You* told me those things, Pierce. *Just now.*"

Pierce shook his head, blanching away from the man across the table. His gaze sharpened, waiting for a punch line. There wasn't one.

Alex produced a black voice recorder from the pocket of his polo shirt, slid it across the table, and pressed play. A crackle turned into a hiss.

Pierce's stomach tightened as he listened, immobile. His voice spat from the device. It was *his* voice, casually divulging his secrets to Frost. Alex placed a calming hand on Pierce's. "I know it doesn't make sense to hear yourself saying this. I can assure you I've not gotten any more secrets than those little codewords. I'm not here to spy on you. You can keep the Dictaphone."

"What did you do then?"

Alex leaned forward again and spoke in a whisper. "I used a technique called neuro-agitation. It's like hypnosis, but light years ahead of it. I also used another technique to produce naturally occurring amnesia to erase our conversation from your memory. Kind of like when you can't find your keys, but they're right in front of you, or when you know the name of a song you hear, but somehow you can't access it. I just took that natural phenomena and made it happen unnaturally around a specific event."

Pierce took in a slow, measured breath, his mind quarreling against this new, apparent reality. "If this—whatever-you-call-it—is real, it seems . . . pretty scary—dark."

"I assure you it's something I could teach to a child in a couple hours. It gets a lot more powerful than that. It's also why you can't lift your right hand. I made it stick to the table in case you decided to punch me or something."

Pierce's eyes flashed down to his hand. He tried to lift it. His bicep strained and his arm shook in protest, but it was stuck. The wooden table had become a new body part. His heart galloped against his chest. Frost looked on, his sympathetic, paternal gaze appraising Pierce.

Alex reached across the table and tapped the back of Pierce's hand. The invisible force fusing it to the table dissolved. Pierce peeled his hand off the table, examining his palm.

"Mister Reston, what I've done here tonight is nothing compared to what I'd like to teach you at our agency." Alex slid a black plastic card across the table with a single phone number on it. "I've spoken to your senior training officer at The Farm, Jim Harrison, old friend of mine. If you decide to join us, he's got a hall pass ready for you." He stood to leave.

"What agency is this? NSA?" Pierce's gaze followed the man up from his seat.

Alex grinned. "I can assure you that you've not heard of us. Give me a call in the next forty-eight hours if you decide you'd like to join us. It's your choice. Also, the two gentlemen seated by the dartboard back there are going to start a fight in about six minutes. They've been quietly arguing with two other guys. The 'tough guy' back there has an inferiority complex that makes him quick to fight—like a scared chihuahua...the most fearful dogs bark the most. The older woman sitting close to the door is going to call the cops." He motioned to a middle-aged woman seated with her husband. "Good night, Mister Reston. I hope to talk soon."

He pivoted and walked out the café's entrance.

Pierce slid the man's card into his pocket, clicked his mechanical pencil, and jotted a note into his book.

> *Alex Frost. ~65, 5'9", 189lbs, grey, tan, blue polo shirt. Cole Haan loafers.*

As he pulled the final sip from his glass, shouting erupted from the rear of the café. The men at the table quarreled at an increasing volume. Pierce didn't look back. Glass shattered on the floor behind him. He stood and walked to the exit. As he passed the short-haired woman near the door, she hissed to the man across from her, "Jesus Christ. This needs to stop now." She snatched up her phone.

Chilly air whipped through his light jacket as he pushed through the exit. His mind strained against this new perception of reality, forcing its way into his understanding of the world.

Deidra burst into Pierce's view, jolting him back into reality. She pointed through the kitchen to the expansive living room beyond. Pierce followed the silent order, striding into the adjacent room. She gestured for him to sit on one of the dark leather couches as an older woman entered the room with a pitcher of coffee and three cups. Deidra thanked the woman and turned to Pierce as he splashed steaming black coffee into one of the shallow cups.

HIG had the pleasure of existing outside the government. The headquarters of HIG was built in, and mostly underneath, a sprawling mansion made up of several buildings that connected underground. The kitchen, which Pierce always believed contained the most advanced equipment in the building, was a work of art. Massive stone walls climbed up to ivory ceilings reinforced with enormous oak beams.

Deidra thanked the woman and continued to brief Pierce as he poured steaming coffee into a cup.

"So, basically, there's a submarine with no crew inside Norfolk Naval Base right now. I've moved our ID station to the driveway, as I'm sure you've seen. We're making you and Kelly multiple sets of identification right now. This has the potential to be a nuclear emergency."

A short beep sounded from the kitchen.

"There's Kelly. I've asked her to come in as well. You guys need to get this sorted as fast as possible."

Kelly's heels clacked on the marble floors as she strode through the kitchen toward the living room. Pierce stood as she approached. She wore a slim-fitting business suit that hugged her hips and a white shirt unbuttoned a third of the way down her chest. Deidra motioned for her to sit. She avoided eye contact with Pierce as she did. Pierce noticed; he assumed Deidra did as well.

Rookie mistake.

Kelly eased into the seat beside Pierce and poured a cup of coffee. "Good morning everyone." She glanced between Pierce and Deidra.

Deidra leaned forward with her hands together. "You two need to get to Norfolk. Kelly, did you read the report?"

"Yes, ma'am. I did," Kelly said, her ponytail bouncing.

“Good,” Deidra said. “Now, onto your priorities. The first priority is determining if there is a rector leak. The Navy guys will probably do all that, but I need that information immediately when they do. Next, I need you to count the missiles. There should be sixteen missiles in the tubes. I’m not concerned with the torpedoes. Finally, where the hell is the crew and what happened to them?”

Kelly adjusted herself further in the seat. She chewed on her lower lip as the monumental size of the mission came to light. Pierce took a sip of coffee and zoomed in on a Norfolk base map on his iPad.

“The guys are printing new IDs for you both in the driveway,” Deidra continued. “You’ll have ID for State Department, Center for Disease Control, and World Health Organization. I’m sending the plane to be on standby at the Norfolk airport; the van will take you down there. The base is on a full lockdown. You need the van and the guards to get onto the base; it’s white-labeled with Department of Defense, so just use your CDC identification to get in, and use your State Department ID to get on the sub.”

“How are we supposed to locate the missing crew? Is there a search going on?” Pierce asked.

“The US government reassured the Russians they are helping, but the Russians continue to assert we killed or kidnapped the sailors. The US Navy is launching a Search and Rescue mission now to scan the area, but I'm not hopeful." Deidra took in a deep breath, her eyes locked in distant contemplation. Pierce and Kelly glanced at each other in a silent exchange.

"To be perfectly honest," Deidra continued, "I don't care if you find the crew. I need to know *how* they disappeared. Test the sub for chemical or biological agents when you're there. I don't care how you have to do it, but you need to get on the sub and have the military test for all that stuff."

"Got it," Kelly said. "What else can we do?"

"Norfolk is forty minutes away. Get prepped on the drive in the sprinter van. They aren't letting people aboard, but they have it tied up at Pier Fourteen at the end of Hughes drive. They evacuated the Aircraft Carrier beside it, as well as all the non-essential personnel on the base, so the whole place should be pretty barren."

"What about protective equipment, and if we need masks or—" Kelly stopped short as Pierce raised a hand.

"We'll find what we need. What is the exact timing on this? Why didn't we detect the submarine coming into the harbor?"

Deidra shook her head. "We don't know much at all." She clicked her tablet on and examined the screen in silence. Kelly's eyes met Pierce's and he shot her a smile that made her visibly relax. Deidra clicked her tablet off and slid it into the seat beside her. She removed her reading glasses and pinched the bridge of her nose. "We were founded to stop war, and this is a worst-case scenario. We're in the dark with this, and we need an all-access pass to what the hell is going on behind the scenes. The other teams are revving up now, but Norfolk is our back yard here. Get your asses on the road now and start filling in these blanks."

Pierce stared at the floor for a moment, eyeing the Persian rug under his feet. Considering. "If one of these missiles is missing..."

Deidra uncrossed her legs and stood. "If a missile is missing, you're going to steal the sub, haul it out of the bay, and sink it in deep water. Caution is no longer on the table."

CHAPTER 3

Washington, DC

Congressman James Frith threw his blazer across the arm of a high-back leather chair as he entered his office. He appraised his office's dark, blue walls, adorned with awards, achievements, and photos of himself with people in power. A large circular rug featuring the seal of The House of Representatives sat perfectly in the center of the room before his desk. He had done well. He extended his arms outward and took in a slow, deep breath.

The news was blowing up over the Russian sub. In thirty minutes, they'd be in the hallway taking interviews on national TV. James would be ready.

His phone buzzed in his pocket. He pulled it out and felt a sobering swell of remorse stab him into reality. Only two words shown on the screen.

The Archer

He swiped the answer button.

"Congressman James Frith," he announced into the phone. He stiffened against the revulsion crawling through him.

"Hello, James. How's the life there in DC?"

"It's been a disaster. The news is exploding around this Russian thing. It's bizarre."

"I can imagine. Hey, I need a favor if you don't mind, James."

The congressman's heart knocked on his rib cage. "Sure, man. What — what can I do for you?" He stepped to his door and prodded it shut.

"I have no doubt you're going on the news soon. You like the spotlight. You look good in the spotlight, I think."

"Y-yeah. I'm going on MSNBC in about thirty minutes. Why?"

"I need your help. We need to make sure this is taken seriously, don't you agree?"

"Well, yes, but I—"

"Me too, James. I need you to suggest a strong military response. The American people need to view this for what it really is. They need to know that this was an *act of war*. Not only does it violate the Geneva Conventions and the Laws of the Sea, but it is an outright sign that we are about to be attacked and we need to take strong, decisive, immediate action."

"Archer, I don't think a crewless submarine poses any threat at the moment. We're mostly worried about the Russian response—what they're trying to suggest we did. We want to work with Russia to make sure—"

"James," the Archer cut him off in a friendly, casual tone. "Strong. Decisive. Immediate action. This is an act of war. An open threat to the American people. Strong. Decisive. Immediate action."

James swallowed his protests. His body brimmed with fury and fear as he echoed the words into the phone. "Strong, decisive, immediate action. This is an act of war. Got it."

"Thanks. Give my best to Karen and the girls."

The line terminated before the congressman could respond.

James walked around his desk and dropped his weight into his leather chair. The photos of himself on the wall stared at him—mocking his plight. He knew he had no choice. No one did when the Archer called.

No doubt later today he would hear those same four words on the news from a dozen other political officials who had made a similar mistake to his own—a damning misstep that left them powerless to the Archer: trusting the man.

Whomever said those precise words today would expose themselves to a small circle of the global elite—subserviently unmasking themselves only to those who knew.

CHAPTER 4

Norfolk, Virginia

The van sped on the shoulder of the road past a line of thousands of cars stuck at a standstill. Kelly wondered if they would make it onto the base at all. Police vehicles, bulldozers, and two HUMVEE trucks with mounted machine guns on the roofs barricaded the naval base's main gate. As the white van neared, the guards, guns, and all attention drew down on it.

The van's driver held out a set of credentials and crept to a stop, feet from the bumper of a white military police vehicle. A nervous sailor clad in a helmet and body armor approached with a hand wrapped around the nine-millimeter Beretta in his thigh holster. He took the papers and stepped back to give the other sailors a clear line of fire in the event the van tried to rush the gate. Kelly stared, amazed at the overwhelming show of force.

The Secretary of Defense had signed the given papers, mandating their entry to the base. The sailor's eyes widened as he stepped back and gave a curt hand signal for the HIG van to proceed. Diesel engines howled as the two HUMVEEs backed up to allow the van through the small opening of the entry point.

The van lurched forward and crossed over the once-forbidden line onto the base. It was a ghost town; not a single vehicle on the streets was visible. The van passed by old brick buildings that looked to Kelly more like an old college campus than a military base. Even the sidewalks were vacant. The HIG driver brought the van to a stop beside the largest ship she'd ever seen. Towering overhead was a gargantuan steel structure that made Kelly shudder. It was ominous and still—a deadly machine bigger than anything she'd ever seen.

"USS *George H. W. Bush*," Pierce murmured.

Kelly's eyes widened. "That's the USS *Bush*?" she said, as she climbed out the side door of the van.

"She is. But you never say the word 'the' before the name of a USS ship. Since it's a name, you just refer to it as you would a person." Pierce, now standing beside her, tossed his sling bag over his shoulder.

Kelly angled her head back to see the ship's deck looming over her. "So . . . That's USS *Bush*?"

"Yep, you got it! Let's go figure out how to get on this sub."

They strolled through the security gate of Pier Fourteen, a set of US State Department credentials hanging around their necks.

A gathering of sprawling, tan military tents was positioned along the pier, each filled with respective agencies and experts. The submarine sat beside the dock. It was solid black and much larger than Pierce imagined. The main upper mast of the sub sat atop the wide body with enormous wings protruding from either side. Just behind that was an extended, raised area that housed the sixteen Russian nuclear missiles. Most of them contained pre-programmed targets in Virginia and DC, set to destroy America.

Something about the stillness of the monster submarine was menacing.

"Holy crap, these things are huuuge," Kelly blurted. She studied the aircraft carrier with her neck craned to search for the top.

"Yeah. Six thousand crew members on a single boat that can do fifty miles an hour. It's insane."

"It's a ship actually." A throaty male voice broke their attention and an approaching man in uniform extended his hand. "Captain Mike Davis. I'm the EOD officer overseeing this operation. You the guys from State Department?"

"That's us," Pierce said, clasping his hand. "I'm Blake Phillips and this here is Valerie Thomas."

The man turned, motioning for the couple to follow. "Glad you guys are here. We are running tests on the sub now. We need to make sure there's no reactor issues or anything. The Secretary of the Navy thinks it might have been some kind of radiation leak that made everyone abandon ship."

They neared a tan tent perched pier side to the submarine. Several sailors stood in green camouflage uniforms before computers and sat on the concrete filling out reports. The humid air pulled at the tent's flaps as they ducked under the edge.

"That's good to hear. How long till you know? And did they actually abandon ship?" Pierce asked.

"We should know in about ten more minutes or so. And no, not really. There's an escape pod designed to fit the entire crew, but it's completely intact. We found something interesting, but we're keeping it classified until we can get some more information." The captain leaned toward Pierce and Kelly. "There *was* a surviving crewmember. He says everyone jumped off into the ocean. Doesn't speak any English."

Kelly squinted. "You mean like suicide? They just jumped off?"

"That's what he says. We think he's lying. He's in a holding cell here on the base. We are testing the air in the sub now with M8 and M9 paper—changes colors if there's chemical or nerve agents onboard. All the initial tests are negative, but the test papers are unreliable; even stuff like cleaning agents can set them off. We are using more equipment now to test for chlorine, cyanide, phosgene gas, and organophosphate pesticides. There're no nerve agents either, but we are still running tests. As far as the nuclear stuff goes, there's nothing. It's as safe as a log cabin in there."

"Thanks, sir," Pierce said. "Is there any way we can get a look inside? State Department wants us to provide Russia with an update immediately."

The captain turned on his heel, beckoning Kelly and Pierce to follow. "I can get you both in there, but you'll need to suit up over there in the station." He jerked his thumb at a decontamination station erected with large PVC pipes and sprawling red tarps spread across the concrete pier. He waved a sailor over and instructed him to suit them up in HAZMAT gear.

At the station, Kelly and Pierce donned SCUBA tanks and large yellow suits. Pierce removed a small testing kit from his pocket and placed it in the outer pocket of the yellow suit. Their faces were covered by full facemasks connected to the SCUBA system, and large yellow hoods slid down onto their heads. The front of the large hood was open, covered only by a transparent face shield. Two sailors finished wrapping tape between their gloves and their suits and the captain approached again, resting a hand on Kelly's shoulder.

"I need you all to stay on the clock here. I'm sending Petty Officer Williams in here with you if you need any help." The captain motioned to a tall sailor wearing a similar suit. "The SCUBA masks have speakers built in, so you shouldn't have to yell. You only have twenty minutes of operational time in there. That tank you have is about an hour and we have to account for the decontamination process. You must keep the mask on during the entire process—that's another twenty minutes or so."

Pierce shot a thumbs up at the captain. "We shouldn't need more time than that. Thanks, Captain!"

"Thanks, Captain. Is my toolkit okay to take into the sub?" Kelly pointed down to a tackle box covered in State Department stickers.

"You bet. You're running out of time, guys. Get in there if you've got work to do."

They crossed a long aluminum walkway and proceeded to step onto the rubbery black surface of the submarine. Petty Officer Williams led the way down a steep ladder into the control room.

Dials, controls, switches, and valves that looked like something from Cold War Russia covered the saffron walls. Kelly inched down the steep decline of the stairs into the sub. "You gotta go down forward on these things; it's actually safer," Pierce called into his microphone.

A few inches of seawater that had apparently accompanied them through the open hatch sloshed at their ankles.

Kelly gripped the handrails as she edged down the ladder. She kept her eyes on the rungs. "You do it your way, *Brent.* I'll do it mine."

The young petty officer chuckled into his microphone.

Kelly stepped off the ladder into control room. Pierce began Tradecraft on the sailor, placing a hand on his shoulder. "*Listen,* Mister Williams, we—*get so turned around*—coming all the way here. You know when—*you try to remember something, and it spins around out of reach*—you can feel it's there but—*there's no way to hear what the memory really is*? There's nothing *here* for you to *hear* when you *feel* the memory of—*this didn't happen—fade out into being right now*—is the perfect time to—*forget—this whole experience*—is a little hazy—is the way I could describe it—begins to notice how much—*you feel completely fine to wait here for me*—while we work?"

After a brief pause, the sailor nodded, the large yellow hood bobbing back and forth. All their SCBA tanks hissed through the shiny suits as they breathed.

Pierce looked back to Kelly and pointed to a painted blue circular opening in the wall. "Kitchen is that way. Go through everything and get samples of everything you can, including the water from the tap and the grease or oil in the fryer, if there is one."

"Got it. Want me to check the dishes? The dirty ones?" Kelly asked. "There might be something."

"Yes. Good call. I'm heading to the oxygen generators. I'll take a few samples as well."

Kelly spun and darted through the opening meant for sailors to go from room-to-room within the sub.

*****

Pierce passed through three circular blue openings and took a left down the second passage beside him. He passed down a flight of stairs and tried to remember how many portals he needed to climb through, thinking back to the diagrams on his iPad.

> *One ladder down, take a left, three portals, open a door.*

Pierce climbed through the third portal, wondering how sailors ran through these things in the movies, and came to a cobalt blue door on his right. The fire-shaped warning icons on the doors confirmed he was in the right place.

ПРЕДУПРЕЖДЕНИЕ! КИСЛОРОД

The oxygen generator was smaller than he'd imagined. On the lower right edge, Pierce spotted the three-stage filter system, and ripped each out of their drawer-like holes. He withdrew a handheld device that looked like a leather hole-punch and clipped a circular section of filter from each of the rectangular devices. He dropped them into a glass tube and slid it into his pocket after wiping the outsides with a cloth dripping with dimethyl benzyl ammonium chloride, sure to kill anything it encountered.

The two rendezvoused back in the submarine's control room. Kelly was speaking very softly into her microphone.

". . . and everything looks good. It all looks good. Everything is totally fine." Her voice grew gradually louder. The entranced Petty Officer Williams slowly came back to consciousness as she continued. "And everything was okay. Thanks so much for your help in the inspection. That went really well; you did a great job. Thank you so much Petty Officer Williams. That was great. Your help with the inspection was really great. We are both so grateful!"

The young man's yellow-hood-covered head bobbed in agreement as he raised a digital stopwatch to his mouth. "We've only got a few more minutes down here. Do you guys need anything else? There might be some kinda gas or something; I'm a little foggy."

"Me too," Kelly announced.

"Roger that," Pierce responded. "Let's get the hell out of this thing. I'm feeling a little weird too."

The trio exited the submarine one at a time, and each was subjected to the required shower that reminded Pierce of washing off a circus elephant—the sailors assisting them scrubbed them down in their plastic suits with push brooms and soap.

Pierce stood still while two other suited sailors removed his protective ensemble one piece at a time. All three were momentarily hooked to a blood pressure and pulse oximeter before being released.

Back at the captain's tent, Kelly briefed the man that they hadn't really found anything. The captain leaned onto a nearby table and wagged his head.

"Since you guys were in there, we got some bad news—just came across the network. Russia is declaring our withholding the submarine an act of war." He withdrew a can of chewing tobacco from a pocket near his calf and tucked a thick pinch of the brown substance into his lip. "The Russians are moving their strike group to our shoreline as we speak. They'll be here in about two days."

CHAPTER 5

Norfolk, Virginia

Back in the van, Kelly and Pierce rode in silence while Kelly typed out an update to HIG on her iPad.

Kelly wondered why the Russian sailors would have jump overboard to their deaths.

"We're going to meet up with Lance Patterson," Pierce said, cutting through the silence. "He and I were in the same class at CIA when I was at the schoolhouse. He's agreed to take the samples here to a lab for covert testing. HIG will get the update in about an hour for the tests."

Kelly's eyebrows shot up. "You have friends?" she gasped.

Pierce ignored her. "We are here." The van pulled into the long driveway of a large brick house.

"Are we going inside?" Kelly asked.

"I hope so. I haven't seen Lance in a long time. He's a great guy. Awesome human being. He's been CIA for about thirteen years now."

The van parked in the driveway and Pierce leaned closer to the two armed men in the front seat. "Could you guys get us a car? I know we needed the van for the base, but we're good. You guys can head back to HIG if you like."

"You bet. I'll have someone drop something off for you guys. Want all your stuff transferred over, Mister Reston?"

"Thank you. That would be perfect. Great job today."

They got out and walked along a white pebble pathway through the perfectly manicured lawn to the front door, which swung open before they could knock.

"Pierce goddamn Reston!"

Lance stood before them with open arms. Pierce hugged the man and introduced Kelly, squeezing her into him as he did. She beamed.

Inside the sprawling house, they sat at a massive wooden kitchen table and Pierce handed the samples across to Lance in a plastic bag sealed with red tape.

"Thanks, guys. I'll have these run immediately for everything—should have results in a few hours when I get them to the lab. It's mostly FBI there, but I have favors that have been burning a hole in my pocket. I'll call them in." Lance turned in his seat and rested the bag on a long, white granite countertop positioned in the center of the orderly kitchen.

Kelly straightened. "What have you heard about the sub so far?"

Lance leaned back in his seat. His chest strained against his flannel shirt as he faced them. "Well, people want to know how the hell this thing even *got* here without us knowing."

"Yeah. Same here," Pierce said.

Lance shook his head. "We have this badass system called IUSS. It stands for Integrated Undersea Surveillance System. It's basically a bunch of cables that run along the bottom of the ocean and listen for stuff underwater all over the world." He pushed his short brown hair out of his eyes. "There's a bunch of them around navy bases, but in the past decade, the number of people who run the program have diminished. Systems got taken offline; people were transferred without replacements. Since the Cold War, the interest level in the IUSS went downhill fast. It was so expensive that other things were prioritized."

Kelly angled her head. "But wouldn't a plane see it? Like, one of the navy's special planes?"

Lance gave Pierce a wide smile. "*Finally*, you're working with someone a lot smarter than you. Yes, Kelly, the planes *can* see subs underwater. But if the sub is below a hundred and fifty feet, there's no chance. It's a little-known secret. That's also the depth these subs have to be at to fire nuclear missiles: fifty meters. Usually, they would have to come up to communicate back to home base, but with ELF communications, they can send messages without having to do that. Extremely Low Frequency waves can penetrate the whole planet, so they could have been down there a long time and gradually drifted to the surface. The sub came in on a high tide, so I think that's what happened."

Pierce grinned. "Wow. I had no idea. I knew you'd know a lot about this, you've been so deep in it for so long. They found one of the younger sailors on the sub, Lance. He says they all jumped ship—like, straight into the ocean. Weird."

"That is weird. Definitely no chemical weapon that can do that. Biological either, come to think of it." He paused and gazed out the kitchen window into the overgrown back yard. "If that's true, then there's something really strange going on. Pierce, let's catch up when you get this wrapped up, man. Been a long time. You and your secret organization can stay secret, but let's at least have a few drinks soon. I'll drive up to Yorktown."

"Indeed, it has. Sorry, man. I'd love to."

Lance stood and snatched the sample bags off the table. "I'll have these back to you in no time. Shoot me a text if you need anything."

Pierce and Kelly exchanged goodbyes with Lance and a Chevy Suburban pulled in behind their van. The men helped Pierce and Kelly load their bags, and they were off.

When Kelly spoke, her voice shook. “What the hell could make an entire crew commit suicide like this if it’s not a weapon? What if it’s Tradecraft like we saw with Phrase Seven?”

Pierce shook his head. “I sincerely doubt it. Tradecraft, even if perfectly crafted, would have taken different amounts of time to work on a whole crew, and sailors who weren’t effected yet would have stopped the others from jumping overboard.” He looked out the window at the passing buildings on Northampton Boulevard. “I’m worried it’s something worse we don’t know about yet.”

CHAPTER 6

Yorktown Virginia

Deidra Collins had already endured three gunshot wounds in Prague and the murder of her friend and mentor, Alex Frost, whom she succeeded as HIG Director. Now, with a looming death toll in the millions, her confidence shrunk with each passing intelligence briefing.

She sat at her wooden desk at the helm of HIG, pouring through documents captured from Russian assets the previous year. There had to be a connection to the submarine incident somewhere, and she was determined to find it. Everything had a connection—if you saw a Saudi Prince humiliated in the news, you'd see a fall in Chinese oil production and eventually a partnership announcement between two unusual companies. Everything was connected. The world was a fabric, and all threads touched each other.

She just needed to find which thread had been pulled.

Under a stack of Manila folders, her phone broke the silence. Deidra felt her way through the folders and found it. She read the screen.

RUASST17

The Russian Asset. Damian.

"Go."

"Ma'am, there's been developments here on this side. The submarine in the US harbor was from Severodvinsk Naval Base. It's in Western Russia near Finland. The Russian Atlantic fleet of submarines are almost all stationed there."

"Copy. Thank you. What's going on over there?"

"Two men died in their apartments last night in Russia. Their bodies were found this morning. They both worked in the shipyard here in Severodvinsk. They worked on many of the submarines here—nuclear and non-nuclear subs. The medical examiner has been restrained from making a public comment, but both men died of radiation poisoning. Russia has halted the deployment of all their submarines until an investigation is complete. They think one of the subs may have a leak in the reactor. Several sailors are showing radiation exposure signs. I don't know how many. Just that they are showing signs."

"Jesus. Who were the two men? What did they do on the submarines?"

"They were Milos Brozovik and Adrej Tusik. Both of them were Serbian nationals. They only lived here in Russia for a couple years. They worked mostly on safety equipment in the submarines. Neither of them had access to the reactor areas inside."

"Well, that doesn't sound right, does it?" Deidra scribbled the names in the margin of a legal pad.

"No, ma'am. I'm looking into it now and I'll keep you posted. And I'm sure you know about Doctor George Finley? The American?"

"I don't. What's up?"

"He was an American bacteriologist. Might not be related at all, but he was reported missing yesterday evening. Well, yesterday evening my time."

"Thank you. Anything else?"

"Not for now, ma'am. I will keep calling with details if I hear anything else."

Deidra terminated the call and gently slid her phone back onto the stack of folders and news reports on her desk. She took in a breath and processed the news, staring at the two names she'd jotted in the margin of her legal pad.

Why would two men from Serbia suddenly die from radiation poisoning?

She took her phone in hand once more and tapped the screen a few times. Before the second ring, Pierce answered.

"Hey, Deidra. We just sent off the samples. Kelly and I are—"

"Pierce, what do you know about Serbia and a potential connection to the Russian Navy?"

"Uh. Well, Russia trained the Serbian military through the nineties. They called it the Slavic Brotherhood. War games and such. Why do you ask?"

Deidra combed through her notes. "Two Serbian nationals were found dead in their apartments today. Both of them worked on the Russian nuclear submarines. Some Russian sailors have potentially been exposed to high levels of radiation. Moscow has put a complete halt on all submarine deployment from Severodvinsk Naval Base. Satellite imagery shows large trucks on the piers adjacent to all the subs as of this morning—probably emergency trucks inspecting for safety. Reactor leaks."

"That's odd. Kelly and I are heading to the airport to get back to HIG. The Navy Captain just called and there's no safety issues with the submarine. They tested for all the common chemical, biological weapons stuff and it all came back negative. We just sent off the samples we took from inside the sub. The sub here in Norfolk is called *Verkhoturye*. K-51. It's a Delta IV class. Carries sixteen holy-shit nuclear missiles, and all of them are safe and sound inside their launch tubes. Kelly got samples from all the food and water supply and they're testing all that too."

Deidra leaned forward onto her desk. "Thanks, Pierce. I got word from the Secretary of the Navy that they are going to try to tow the sub out to sea in case something is amiss. I need you and Kelly to get to Severodvinsk Naval Base and figure this out. We have a missing bacteriologist here in the US, two dead Serbians, and a recall of all Russian subs. The Russian fleet should be on our eastern border in a couple of days."

"Don't we have assets in Russia?"

Deidra stared aimlessly at the floor as she thought about it. "Well, they are only assets. We don't have operatives I can send into the base at a moment's notice. Go out there. Take Kelly. And bring a jacket. It's about fifty-five degrees there right now."

She waited through a moment of silence.

"Yes, ma'am. We're fifteen minutes from the airport. I'll call the jet now to prep."

CHAPTER 7

Norfolk, Virginia

Kelly looked over her shoulder and spun the wheel. "We can be at the airport in about ten. We'll go behind the outlet mall."

Pierce hung up the phone and reclined in his seat. He flicked through intelligence documents Deidra sent to his iPad and came to rest on a Serbian national named Milos Brozovik, one of the men who died of radiation poisoning. He turned to Kelly as she flicked on the turn signal. "Listen to this. Milos Brozovik—Serbian from Belgrade. He gets a job on the Russian naval base checking labels on basic safety equipment like life jackets, fire extinguishers, and such. Three years prior, he earns a doctoral degree in microbiology. How does that sound to you?"

Kelly kept her eyes on the road and shook her head. "Sounds like a surgeon becoming a janitor.

Then the guy just suddenly dies of radiation poisoning?"

"Yeah. Not buying it. His behavior profile is driven by a feeling of significance and a need to impress others. This isn't normal behavior. The other guy who died—this guy was a welder in Belgrade. Both are from Belgrade. Both took jobs to clean and update safety equipment on Russian naval bases." Pierce scratched his cheek. A notification flashed onto the screen from Deidra—a video file.

"Do you speak Russian? I don't. Never been to Russia, actually." Kelly shrugged. "This should be interesting."

"Deidra sent a video. It's from the news." Pierce clicked on the file to find US Congressman James Frith voicing his frustration.

"This is an act of war!" the congressman shouted into the camera. "Our interests *have* to be rooted in national security. They brought a nuclear submarine loaded with nuclear missiles into our naval harbor. We can't afford to wait and see what they do next. We need to take *strong, decisive, immediate action*."

Pierce's eyebrows narrowed as he watched the video. Kelly pulled the Suburban into the private terminal of the Norfolk International Airport and threw it into park.

"Look at this," Pierce said, pointing a finger at the screen. "His neck. Do you see it?"

He rewound the video and the congressman's voice came through the iPad once more. "Our interests have to be rooted in national security. They brought a nuclear submarine into our naval harbor loaded with nuclear missiles. We can't wait and see what they do next. We need to take *strong, decisive, immediate action."*

Kelly straightened, eyes squinted. "I don't get it. I saw a micro- expression of fear several times throughout the video."

Pierce tapped the screen. "Look again at the sternocleidomastoid muscles—"

"Fear," Kelly breathed. "His whole body is tensing."

"Protecting every artery," Pierce finished, nodding. "Great for sabretooth tigers a long time ago, but pretty sloppy for concealing emotions today. He thinks he's in danger."

"Why?" Kelly shot Pierce a glance before looking back at the screen. "Wow. Even his shoulders are raised. That's pure fear—like, full-body fear."

Kelly watched in silence as Pierce played the video and studied the screen for a minute. After watching it a third time, he clicked the iPad off and plopped it onto the seat. "He's either nervous about the consequences of speaking his mind or someone has forced him to say those words—and I've never seen this man afraid to speak his mind."

"That's the triangle Alex always talked about," Kelly said. "Transparency, Courage, and Integrity."

Pierce nodded. "No politician will ever have all three sides. Every politician will be missing one leg of the triangle, and that's their weak point. Even when they adopt a third leg, another deteriorates."

Kelly flipped on the turn signal. "We're here. Let's get to Russia."

CHAPTER 8

Washington, DC

Vincent Braid cinched the knot on a cobalt tie and checked his reflection in the bedroom mirror. The diplomats from Germany would be arriving any minute. He didn't much enjoy these visits, but as was tradition, when NATO countries visited, the vice president would invite them to his home for lunch. With the current crisis, Braid halfway assumed the Germans would cancel and he'd be able to return to the White House to keep the president from making stupid decisions.

He had only been in office for a year and already felt the tremendous weight beginning to eat through what he'd thought was thick skin. His hair had turned grey in his brief time moving up the ladder in DC.

His wife ambled into the room, affixing an earring to her ear, and positioning herself in front of a full-length mirror on the adjacent wall. "God, I hope they don't stay long. Why would they still want to meet with this stuff going on with Russia?"

"I don't know, darling. They may offer their version of help for this crisis. Last time the Saudis and Russians had issues, they came knocking, wanting to be some kind of mediator."

Braid threw on his jacket. His phone began chiming a staccato tone he knew all too well. He peered over his shoulder to see his wife still fiddling with her earrings and stepped out of the room. Glancing down at the screen, he recoiled.

Belgrade Archer

He clenched his teeth.

This isn't the time for whatever this little shit has in mind. He has the balls to call my cell phone in the middle of all this.

He dragged a reluctant finger across the answer button and pressed the phone to his ear. "Hey. What gets you up at this hour?" Braid's teeth clamped down in protest.

"Vince, it's evening over here. How's the family?" The ominous, charming voice sent an all-too-familiar chill through his body.

"Everyone's fine. Just fine. What—can I do for you? I should just call you Archer on the phone, right?"

"Yes, thank you. You're a strong man, Vincent. Extraordinarily strong. Would you agree with that?"

"What is this about, Archer?"

"Well, *I* agree with that. You've done so much for the country. I just need you to maintain your strength. This situation can get out of hand quick without someone decisive at the helm. You've been the one guiding the hand of the president. I need you to treat this incident with the sub as what it is."

Vince's jaw tightened into a rock. "And what might that be?"

"Well, I'm no Rhodes Scholar, but according to your own laws, this qualifies as an act of war, Vincent."

Braid balked at the man's tone. "Some people think so."

"Well, we all have opinions. I hope you agree with those people. This is something you need action on. Something that will guarantee your reelection as well. An act of war means a strong response. You're strong, and it would be appropriate to respond in kind to this blatant intrusion on American soil with proportional action. Military force."

Vince peered through the blinds, checking to see if the German delegates had shown up. "Why the hell would I possibly—"

"Vince, I have tremendous faith you'll exercise your judgment and come to the same conclusion.

An act like this warrants a response with force. What I'd like to see is strong, decisive, immediate action. Strong, decisive, immediate action. Do you need a pen?"

"I don't." Braid repeated the phrase like a reprimanded child. "Strong, decisive, immediate."

"Action, Vince. Action."

Braid took a deep breath, centering himself. "Action."

"Thanks, Vince. You're a brilliant vice president. A wonderful leader. Give my best to Kathryn."

Braid swam through nauseating memories; a filth he could never escape. He straightened his back against the crippling shame in his belly. He tramped across the room to his antique desk, withdrew a golden pen, and slid a pad of paper toward him with a finger. After a short pause, he jotted four words with a now-shaking hand.

strong decisive immediate action

CHAPTER 9

GeopoliticalTimes.com

BREAKING NEWS

DID THE US 'KIDNAP' A RUSSIAN SUBMARINE?

The Russian nuclear submarine Verkhoturye *sits tied to a pier in Norfolk as the world looks on. Initial reports, and video from several American sailors on social media, have shown so far that there is no crew aboard the submarine* Verkhoturye.

As the two superpowers struggle to navigate the situation, tensions across America have risen, with a massive increase in military and defense stocks and hour-long waits at gas stations across the country.

Russia is accusing the US of capturing the submarine. In an official statement this morning from the Joint Chiefs of Staff, General Spaulding says that "… the United States has not had an ounce of involvement in this tragedy. We are working closely with Russia as they continue to escalate tensions. For the time being, it's important we take strong, decisive, immediate action in order to keep our country secure."

CHAPTER 10

Arkhangelsk Oblast, Russia

Neither of the HIG pilots spoke Russian, and the ground control tower of the tiny airport was staffed with entirely Russian-speaking personnel.

After two fueling stops, the Gulfstream GV banked hard left toward the Vaskovo Airport. Pierce strode down the carpeted aisle to the cockpit, allowing his eyes to adjust in the dark. Hundreds of tiny gauges and switches threw a faint glow onto the pilots. Ahead, the lights of the small Russian town cast orange light into the thin clouds. He placed a hand on the captain's shoulder.

The pilot pulled off an earpiece of his headset and leaned toward Pierce. "We're going to phone into HIG to let them translate the radio calls for us," he shouted over the hum of the engines.

The pilot held his phone into his headset microphone, allowing HIG staff to translate his radio calls to and from the tower over the speaker.

The plane's radio fizzed with indecipherable Russian commands.

The pilot wiped beads of sweat from his forehead and stared at his cell phone. A few seconds later, a man's voice chirped through the phone with a perfect translation. "Nordwind Private 387 cleared to land runway right, wind 035 degrees, eight knots, maintain heading three zero."

The pilot turned back to Pierce, silently mouthing, *Holy shit*.

The plane bounced onto the narrow runway moments later. Pierce pivoted to Kelly. Her black, slim-fitting business attire complemented his own dark grey suit. She had slicked her hair back into a cute ponytail that brought the angles of her jawline into focus.

Pierce's phone buzzed on the dark wood table in front of him.

Deidra Collins

He put the phone on speaker. "Just landed."

"I know. Listen, we got results back from the samples you guys took. Nothing unusual, but they did find toxoplasma in the water samples Kelly obtained from the kitchen. Kelly?"

Kelly leaned toward the phone. "Yes, ma'am?"

"Where did you take the water samples?"

"There were three sinks in the kitchen—er, galley area. I took a sample from each of those and a few from some dirty dishes. There was one coffee mug, but it looked too clean to check."

"Okay. They all tested positive for *Toxoplasma gondii*."

Kelly's face twisted. "Like the bacteria in cat pee?"

"Yes," Deidra growled. "But it's not bacteria, it's a parasite. It's found in contaminated meat as well. Still, there's no way this can be the reason. We also found out the two men who died of radiation poisoning had no signs of hair loss or anything else. The experts here tell me it had to be a quick death. They could have been messing with the reactor, maybe caused some kind of leak. I need you both to see if the Russians are involved. Two Russian AIG intelligence-gathering ships are positioned just outside Norfolk now. The Russian fleet is about eight hundred nautical miles out. They'll be on our shores in forty-eight hours."

"Dammit." Pierce pulled his iPad from his bag. "I'm looking at the intel you sent over. The Serbian men died in their homes, not on the base. They were also the only Serbian workers in the shipyard—both of them recently hired. Sounds like this may not be a radiation leak on the subs at all."

"That's right, Pierce. Get me more info. Get on that sub and get samples to our local asset. He's waiting for you at the terminal building. It's only a half-hour drive to Severodvinsk from there. If terrorists contaminated the subs, we need to alert the Russian government. As for the two Serbians—find out what the hell happened."

The plane jerked to a stop west of the terminal building. Pierce and Kelly wheeled their oversized equipment bags through the terminal, flashing their white Diplomatic passports to the two men at the security desk. Neither of them bothered to stand.

The local asset, Viktor, was a twenty-year-old kid who had acquired a large passenger van. The young Russian was dressed in a way that Pierce had assumed was a stereotype—an Adidas track suit. He pushed his short hair back as he introduced himself to Kelly and Pierce in broken English. He grabbed both handles of their bags and hefted them into the back of the van.

Kelly's eyebrows darted upward. She leaned into Pierce and whispered, "Scout?"

HIG had a knack for recruiting loyal assets, known as Scouts. Viktor was no exception. HIG agents recruited people from all corners of the globe. Over the course of a week, using what HIG called 'Long-Form Tradecraft,' an operative could essentially program someone to be on call whenever they were needed. Once an asset was programmed, they were fiercely loyal and always at the ready to execute any given command.

Pierce nodded with a grin. A HIG operative would serve as the Scout's handler—ensuring they were taken care of and that their programming didn't wear off over time. Every Scout could be put into action using an activation phrase their handler assigned to them during programming.

He extended his hand to the asset. "Hi! Pierce and Kelly. Forest, Jupiter, Nine." He lowered his tone with each word.

Viktor's body relaxed. His pupils enlarged and he straightened back up, introducing himself in only slightly broken English. "Good to meeting you both!" He opened the van's rear door for them. "Welcome to Russia! We are only maybe thirty kilometers from Severodvinsk. You want music on radio?"

Before Pierce could tell the Scout they wanted peace and quiet after the long flight, Kelly shot upright. "Yes! Put on some really good Russian music!"

Pierce suppressed a sigh. Kelly sat back in her seat, smiling, making him wonder if he'd become grumpier with age.

An enthusiastic Viktor leapt into the driver's seat and pulled the van out of the parking lot. He leaned forward and punched a button on the radio. The peaceful silence was broken by angry Russian rap music. Kelly covered her mouth and smiled at Pierce through her fingers.

After a forty-minute drive, Viktor squeezed the van into a tight parking spot at a small convenience store. “Okay. Navy base is there,” he said, motioning out the windshield.

Pierce turned on his iPad and zoomed in on the apartment building where one of the Serbians had died. “Can you take us here? How far is this?”

Viktor squinted at the display. “Yes. This is on Prospekt Truda. Only two minutes. This building is where the Serbian guy’s body was found.”

Pierce nodded for him to drive.

Minutes later, the van entered a parking space at 16 Prospekt Truda. Kelly leaned forward, peering through the window at the run-down grocery store in front of them.

“What’s this, Viktor?”

“This is apartment. Here you show me *this* on iPad.” Viktor pointed up through the windshield.

Pierce followed his finger’s trajectory into the dimly lit street. The four floors above the store were an apartment building. Decaying walls and dingy windows lined the building. “Well, this is it. Let’s see if we can get some answers. Kelly, you have your W.H.O. ID card?”

Kelly nodded and recovered it from the backpack beside her. “Viktor, come on inside with us. We only need to see if there is anything amiss up there. Apartment 418."

A chilly breeze whipped down the street as they exited the van. Pierce looked down at his suit with a grimace. Street clothes would have been a much better choice. They walked past the grocery store to the entrance to the apartments above, where a Middle Eastern man sat on a plastic lawn chair reading a paper.

Viktor nodded at the man. "*Gde ya mogu nayti kvartiru 418?*"

Without as much as a glance, the man gestured to a staircase to their left.

They reached the fourth floor, Viktor leading the way. They passed by several apartment doors. A blaring Russian television show and the cries of a grumpy baby filled the dingy, yellow hallway. They continued on, the smell shifting between mothballs and Asian noodles.

"Here. 418!" Viktor strolled up to a door sealed by black tape with white letters printed on it.

ПОЛИЦИЯ - НЕ ВХОДИТЕ

He tapped on the police tape across the entrance. Viktor leaned toward Kelly, motioning to the tape with his head. "Know what this says here?"

"Stay the fuck out?" Kelly said.

"You got it! You are *very* good at Russian." He laughed at his joke as he pushed the door open and ducked under the tape. "The police took the body this morning."

The syrupy, rotten-egg smell of death enveloped them as they pushed the tape aside. It looked abandoned. Kelly's arm shot to her face, filtering her air from the smell crawling from the apartment. The narrow hallway led to a small, empty kitchen with peeling, green wallpaper. A tiny folding card table sat in the corner, chairless. On the table, a single notepad and pen.

Every cupboard was empty, save for three boxes of energy bars, packages of ramen noodles, and a case of bottled water. The connected bedroom contained one mattress covered in blankets and a chair, presumably from the kitchen. Next to the bed, a faded blue sheet covered up a small lump on the floor. Pierce strode over to the sheet and threw it back. On the floor was a stiff, dead cat that had been tossed into its litter box.

"Who the hell would do something like this?" Kelly spun toward the exit, holding her stomach.

"You are new to Russia. Russian Police don't care about animals," Viktor said, lighting a cigarette.

Clumps of cat fur had fallen into the litter box around it, and an equally sizeable amount of fur was strewn across the bed.

Pierce pulled his wallet open and slid out a business card. He tore off a long strip of the thick white paper and placed the rest back into his wallet. He knelt beside the dead cat and slid the edge of the strip into the cat's mouth, working it back and forth. "We can send this off for testing, too. Kelly, what's on the notepad in the kitchen?"

Kelly trotted back into the kitchen.

Pierce stood over the dead cat. "Viktor, hand me the wrapper from your cigarette pack."

Viktor slid the wrapper off his pack of Marlboro and handed it over to Pierce, who inserted the business card strip and rolled the plastic around it, tucking it in his jacket pocket.

"Guys, we maybe don't have lot of time here." Viktor flicked his cigarette ashes onto the brown linoleum floor.

Pierce nodded and walked to the kitchen where Kelly stood over the notepad on the table. "Anything?"

"Something was written here. Maybe we can use a pencil and rub it on there to read it?'

Pierce grabbed the notepad off the table and inspected it. "You have your phone?"

Kelly reached into her breast pocket. "Yep."

Pierce laid the notepad down on the table. "Shine the flashlight directly from the side of the notepad here. The indentions will make shadows, but we won't be able to see them...yet."

Kelly scrunched her face. “Okay?”

Pierce took out his phone and she illuminated the notepad from the side. Pierce took a photo of the paper from above and showed Kelly. “See?”

“Uh. No? It looks like regular old paper.”

“Exactly. But the shadows are there.” Pierce opened the photo editor and adjusted the brightness and contrast. The writing appeared on the paper in faint lines.

“That’s badass,” Viktor said, peering over Pierce’s shoulder.

“Yeah. Agreed,” Kelly said, shooting a doting smile at Pierce.

“It looks like an account number. Write this down, Kelly. RS35160005400003088383.”

“That’s IBAN. International Bank Account Number,” Viktor offered through a smoky exhale.

Pierce snapped a few photos of the dead cat and they left the building. Viktor started driving and Pierce sent the images to HIG. In under a minute, Mariel Thomas, the Senior Operations Officer, called Pierce.

She didn’t wait for Pierce to say hello. “Pierce, which house was that cat in?”

“One of the Serbians. Milos Brozovik.”

“Okay. We have our team looking now. The cat looks like it has also died from radiation. The tongue is black, and the hair is falling out. Did you notice anything else about it? Was there vomit?”

"Yeah. Like a yellowish color where all the hair was on the bed."

Viktor turned right onto Karla Marksa toward the navy base.

"Pierce. There's no radiation leak on the sub. There's something else going on. The last sub these guys were on. What was it?" Mariel asked.

"*Belgorod*!" Viktor interrupted, sitting up straighter in his seat. "It's a new Oscar-class nuclear submarine. It's here in the shipyard. It's one of the new subs. It's in the documents you sent to me this morning."

"Was that the Scout?" Mariel shot, after a moment of silence.

"Yes. What do you need from us, Mariel?"

"Both of you need to focus on finding out *how* these two Serbians died. Get onto the naval base. I need everything you can get me from the sub. We are still running the toxoplasma. Something isn't right about it. Get samples of the sub's water, at a minimum."

"Thanks, Mariel. We will go in tonight." Pierce ended the call and faced Kelly.

"So, all we have to do is infiltrate a heavily guarded Russian nuclear submarine base, then somehow get on board unnoticed and sneak *back* out with the samples."

Viktor blew a stream of smoke out the window and chuckled. "They will kill you both."

CHAPTER 11

Moscow, Russia

The young woman kneeling in front of him interrupted his train of thought. She angled a make-up brush toward his face. "Admiral, just one more spot I'd like to get here. Your forehead will be shiny on camera if I don't."

He offered a curt nod as she leaned in and blotted his forehead with the brush. Cameras and crew for the national news network filled his office. A taller cameraman adjusted a wooden model of a submarine on his desk. The woman made a final adjustment to his short grey hair. Every time he adjusted in his seat, her hand yanked backward so as not to interfere with his movement. Dimitri scanned the room. The camera crew clumsily avoided eye contact. His reputation was reflected in the shrinking postures of the people around him.

Admiral Dimitri Kostyukov had seen his country endure a transition into corruption at the hands of the Americans. The Soviet way of life was what made his country great. Now, his Navy and his ships were at the mercy of political pressure, oil prices, and incessant arguments with soulless Saudis that inevitably wound up with Russia capitulating to their demands.

As a KGB officer, he had earned the right to kill for his country. Now, as the Russian Fleet Admiral, he commanded the Navy, but his powers to kill for his country were more diminished than ever. The Kremlin kept a tight grip around his neck. He knew the war would come; he had spent a lifetime preparing for it.

In less than two days, his fleet would descend on the Americans and the world would know the truth. *Russia* was the reason the world was safe.

A woman's voice pierced the muted bustle in his small office. "We are live in twenty seconds, sir."

The admiral straightened in his seat and adjusted the earpiece connecting him to the news studio in Moscow. He adjusted his dress uniform one last time.

Bright lights clicked on in front of his desk, illuminating him from just beyond the camera.

After a short burst of static, his earpiece sparked to life. ". . . and that's the reason we've brought Admiral Kostyukov here with us today. He's joining us from his office in the Central

Command. Admiral Kostyukov is the Fleet Admiral of Russia and oversees all naval operations. His forty-year career has spanned seventeen combat tours and thirty-nine peace campaigns around the world. Admiral, can you give us any insight on the situation with the Americans?"

Kostyukov gazed squarely into the camera and nodded. There was a two-second delay, so he'd need to begin answering the question as the reporter finished speaking. The Americans would take any chance they could to point out technical difficulties, citing them as evidence of Russia's inferiority.

"Thank you, Ivan. The situation with the submarine is both tragic and telling of our current times. Our relationship with The United States has decayed to a point where they have captured one of our submarines and created a common American smoke screen regarding the location of our beloved sailors. The Americans have awoken in all of us a realization that their greed has no end. I can only hope the country joins me this evening in prayer for our sailors. Unprovoked, America has launched into what can only be seen as an act of war."

The admiral leaned forward to the camera. "These are the absolute facts. Unprovoked, they have decided to keep a Russian submarine captive. As you know, we never ask for war, but we will not stand by while our great country is torn apart the same way we see the Americans tear apart other countries—from the inside out. The Americans will have a tough decision tonight. Consequences catch up to us all, and perhaps it is time for lessons to be learned by the schoolyard bully."

CHAPTER 12

Severodvinsk Naval Base, Russia

Kelly unzipped her pants in the back of the van and slid them off. Earlier, Viktor had taken them to a local pawn shop, Lombard's. They were able to secure two fitting sets of Russian Navy Coveralls: the uniform worn by all the local sailors. Pierce watched the rear-view mirror, ensuring Viktor kept his eyes forward.

The van navigated the dark streets of Severodvinsk toward the ocean. Pierce zipped the dark blue coveralls over his slim-fitting body armor.

As the sun set over the town, Pierce concealed the last bit of a body-worn antenna around his waist that resembled a long, rubber-coated electrical cord. He fought against his increasing worry for Kelly. Russian broadcasters continued a shouting match through the van's radio. Viktor wove his way around potholes as Pierce pulled out a grey hard-shell case and withdrew two bright yellow taser guns from foam cutouts.

“There’s no way we can hurt these people. No matter what. Even if they try to kill us, our maximum level of force in response will be to knock them out.” He handed a stun gun to Kelly.

They retrieved their aluminum clipboards from their bags. Each clipboard opened to reveal a storage area beneath where papers could be stored. They fit the tasers inside, along with their radios, a roll of cotton swabs, a knife, and a roll of small plastic bags for the samples.

Kelly leaned toward Pierce. “If we can prove Russia isn’t involved in this, what’s the next step?”

“The next step is finding who *is* responsible and handing their head on a plate to the Russians. Both of our country’s propaganda machines are spinning at full speed right now. Ours is only slightly more subtle. At least Russia openly *admits* that their government controls the media.”

Pierce and Kelly walked through their plan a final time on the iPad.

Viktor tilted his head and peered into the rear-view mirror. “Okay. You will need to go on foot to the north pier once we stop. It’s a nice walk on the beach. You’re lucky for good weather now here. Other times of year is all snow and ice.”

“Thanks, Viktor. Where’s the entrance from here?”

"Only maybe two minutes. We are going to west side of the base to the beach. This road here, Severo Zapadnaya, leads to the northwest of base. There is no security. The tugboats in the harbor are not really tugboats. They are security. They will have big spotlights on them and usually three men with AK47s. In back of the dock area where the submarine is sitting, there is only one guard most of the time, also with AK47. They have a lot of trucks around the submarines. Lots of people inspecting them. I use a very nice camera drone from the beach for this."

"Thanks, Viktor." Pierce and Kelly turned on their radios and looped the translucent earpieces behind their ears.

Mariel's voice came through within seconds. "*Privet, rebyata!*"

"Your Russian isn't too bad!" Kelly sang into her mic.

"I had to look it up online. I practiced it a couple of times. How's it going?"

"Hey, Mariel," Pierce said. "We're on Severo-Zapadnaya Ulitsa now. Passing a row of storage units that were converted into business shops. We are going to the west side of the base and have about an eight-minute walk to the edge of the submarine piers. Kelly is going to take point. We still don't know how the guards standing watch are positioned."

The van slowed and Viktor came to a gentle stop at the end of a sandy pathway leading to the beach a hundred yards away. “I will pick you up here, but I have my phone if you need to change location.”

“Thanks, Viktor. We shouldn’t be more than an hour. We’ll keep you posted.” Pierce patted the man on the shoulder and exited the van with Kelly.

The two walked in the quiet darkness in their Russian uniforms, clipboards held close to the chest, for nine minutes along the beach. A cold northern wind whipped sand into the air. The smell of ocean and marine life was thick and laced with diesel.

“If anything happens, don’t lose the samples. According to the satellite images, there’s a break in that sea wall that opens to the submarine dock right here.” Pierce pointed to a narrow split in a tall white sea wall on their right. They navigated the dark, grassy beach and came to the narrow passage. No one was there. They passed through the opening onto the long concrete dock extending to the east. Only two hundred yards ahead of them, two long, black submarines sat beside each other. Large cables tied them both to the pier and each other. The wall to their left dampened the effects of the northern wind.

Pierce clicked his mic. “Two guards. Armed. Twelve o’clock. Let’s keep at least forty feet of separation in case one of us is spotted.”

"Check. I'm hanging back. I'll be on your six at forty feet." Kelly's soft voice swept a wave of calm through Pierce. He tucked the metal clipboard under his arm and stayed in the shadows cast from large, rusty shipping containers dotting the pier.

The rumble of an engine drew his attention to his right. In the dark, a rusty tugboat drew closer to the two submarines. A bright white light shone on the surface of the water near the two subs and crept upward, inspecting the sides of the long submarine.

Pierce whispered into his mic, "We've got one security boat in the harbor here. Looks like three guys on board. One driving, two armed topside. The sub we're looking for is on the outboard side from the pier. We'll have to cross over the first sub to get to it."

"Copy all. I see it. It's different than the one in Norfolk."

Mariel's voice crackled into the earpiece. "This one is brand new, guys. It's the newest Oscar-Class submarine. The Belgorod sub was converted for spy missions. She can even launch robots out the top. It's a *lot* bigger. It's actually the longest submarine in the world. You need to be in and out in about fifteen minutes."

"Got it. Looks like one more guard on the sub itself. We've got activity just beyond this truck." Pierce crouched behind a parked truck on the pier and angled his body to align with the shadows.

Kelly tucked into the darkness behind a shipping container. "Two guards on the pier here at the walkway to cross onto the sub."

"There's too much movement on the pier. Fall back ten yards and wait. We'll need to use the aft morning line to get aboard." Pierce spun without a sound and stayed low as he crept toward a large, rusted mooring cleat that the sub's morning lines were looped around, tying it to the shore. "Kelly, hang back and keep overwatch. There're too many people here for us to go in blind with no one keeping a lookout. I'm going to have to slide across this mooring line."

"Line?"

"Rope."

"Oh. Got it."

"Wait for the tugboat to finish this pass. When they turn outbound, I'm going across. Keep me posted on security and movement outside the sub. I'll get the samples."

"Got it. Moving back to point Charlie." They'd established the overwatch position on the shipping containers using high-resolution imagery of the base. After a short pause, Kelly chirped in his earpiece. "I'm at Charlie, Pierce, on top of the container. Going to lay as flat as I can. I'll keep you posted on movement. The tug is turning outbound."

The tug's spotlights shifted away from the submarines as it turned to the right, engines roaring. Pierce knelt beside the large steel cleat and leaned over the water. He gripped the large, tightly wound rope leading to the back of the submarine with both hands and dropped his weight off the pier. Dangling in the dark, Pierce pulled his legs up slowly and wrapped them around the mooring line, crossing his ankles. Hanging upside down, he inched his way to the unlit rear of the submarine.

"Pierce. The guard on the sub is headed back your way. He's holding a flashlight."

Pierce lengthened his body along the mooring line to minimize his silhouette. The Russian sailor approached the rear of the first submarine with an AK47 rifle casually slung across his shoulder.

The sailor aimed the flashlight into the water as he took a drag of a cigarette and flicked it into the sea. He walked away toward the nose of the sub. Pierce sprung back to life and continued to climb the taut, woven line hanging upside down, his clipboard tucked into his coveralls.

He reached the rear of the second sub and dropped his feet below him. Only a foot below, the sub's partially submerged tail fins spread out wider than the wingspan of a 747. The thing was an engineering marvel. Pierce let go of the rope and splashed into the shallow water covering the fins. He turned to the main body of the submarine and continued forward in a low crouch, keeping every part of his body within the confines of shadows and darkness. He neared the towering control mast in complete silence, then came to an abrupt stop, seeing a puff of cigarette smoke drift from just beyond the front.

"There's one more guard here. Armed," Pierce whispered.

"Copy. If the tug keeps schedule, they'll be back in about eight minutes."

Keeping low, Pierce edged to the rear the control mast and peered around the corner. The entrance of the submarine was at the base of the tall mast section, and a tent covered the opening. A heavy, steel, watertight door laid open, exposing a staircase descending into the sub. Pierce took a single step forward, now exposed under the lights.

Beyond the tent, an older sailor stood with his rifle slung across his body, rubbing his hands together against the cold. Pierce darted under the canopy toward the man in a crouch. Just behind the sailor, he sprung upward. With one hand, Pierce secured the barrel of the rifle, maintaining control of the man using the rifle sling. With the other hand, he covered the man's nose and mouth. He yanked the sailor off balance and spun to the left, jerking him off his feet and into the darkness. Using the hand covering the man's face, Pierce slammed his head onto the deck.

The man's body fell into a relaxed mass, and he began to snore. Pierce gripped the man's collar, hauled the rest of his body into a dark shadow and disabled his rifle.

“Guard on this sub is down. Going in.”

Pierce’s phone buzzed in the breast pocket of his coveralls. He removed it, careful to cover the light from the screen.

No Caller ID. Probably Viktor.

Pierce answered. “What’s up?”

“Hello! We’ve been trying to reach you about your car’s extended warranty! Press one now to—”

“Fucking hell.”

He stabbed the phone back into his pocket and descended the steep metal staircase into the depths of the machine. The yellowish walls looked a lot more modern than the sub in Norfolk did, covered in digital control devices and flat screen monitors for all the sub’s vital signs.

“I’m inside. I’ll lose comms until I’m out.”

Walking briskly down the narrow passageway, passing gauges, pipes, switches, and valves all labeled in Russian, he descended another staircase to the second level of the submarine into another yellow passageway. After thirty more steps, as Mariel had advised, he saw the one word in Russian he had learned to spot: *КАМБУЗ*, the galley.

Pierce swung open the heavy steel door to find a large, empty kitchen. The loud hum of the ventilation system filled the room. The smell of stale cabbage and cleaning supplies encircled him. The blue-tiled floor was different than the rest of the submarine, which was translucent epoxy. He crept to a stainless steel-covered dishwashing area in the left rear corner and twisted the handle on the sink, slipped a glass vial from his pocket, and filled it with the water that sprang from the faucet. He screwed the lid down tightly, and wiped the remaining water from the tube and his hands with an anti-microbial cloth. He returned the tube to the clipboard, and ran a cotton swab across the stoves, sinks, and ventilation ducts.

As he closed the lid of the clipboard, the heavy kitchen door swung open, smacking against the stainless-steel wall behind it. Pierce dove behind the sink and drew his taser from his kit. The sound of the ventilation system prevented him from hearing anything.

"*Kto zdes'?*" an angry voice shouted into the galley. "*Kto zdes'?*"

Pierce stayed crouched behind the sink. To his right, a giant Russian sailor's leg was visible under the sink. The man spun, walking around the sink. Pierce slid on his knees, latched his arms around the man's legs, and yanked as hard as he could. As he expected, the man's torso smacked the deck with enough force to rattle kitchen equipment hanging nearby.

Tearing to the side, Pierce flipped him over and slid onto his back, wrapping an arm around his neck and holding it tightly with the other. The heavy sailor kicked off of a steel table, slamming Pierce backward into the base of a stove that was bolted to the floor. Pain flashed through his neck and shoulders; violent, burning agony exploded up from his spine to the top of his head.

He held a firm grip on the sailor's neck, squeezing until his arms shook. Massive fists swung back, delivering wild blows and bursts of pain to the side of Pierce's head. Within seconds, however, the man's titan body loosened into a pile on the polished kitchen deck.

Pierce stood, probed through his hair for blood, picked up the clipboard kit, and shot through the door. Inside the passageway, two more sailors in coveralls walked together, ascending the ladder Pierce needed to use. He followed them, keeping his distance, his heart still thundering. On the staircase, he leaned to examine the passageway above. Empty. He climbed the steps and sprinted toward the exit.

As he turned toward the stairs to exit the sub, his radio began receiving again. Kelly was in the middle of a transmission. ". . . probably thirty of them. Pierce isn't out yet."

He clicked his mic. "I'm out. At the main hatch."

"Stop there, Pierce. Stop!" Kelly cried. "They found the guy you knocked out. There are about twenty of them heading your way now!"

CHAPTER 13

London, England

Nuclear outbreak was now a real possibility.

Johnathan James laid alone in bed after another day of non-stop negotiation between the Americans and the Russians.

As the Secretary of State for Defense, Johnathan served at Her Majesty's pleasure. His duties, however, were to report to the Prime Minister, a man who seemed hell-bent on imposing the Armed Forces of the United Kingdom in the Russian submarine event. Johnathan had no interest in involving Her Majesty's Royal Navy in this dick-measuring contest. Not only would it inflame Russia's sensitive ego, but it would also most certainly escalate the already heightened tension.

His bedroom ceiling seemed lower than usual. Closer to him. He eyed the room around him, peering over his glasses. The white, oversized crown molding and blue-trimmed decorative striping led downward to a collection of paintings and artwork that rivaled the Leighton House Museum in London.

Despite his home's opulence, it felt like a shrinking cage, limiting his thoughts, his movement, his freedom. All reminding him he wasn't really in charge.

Johnathan removed his reading glasses and set them on top of a folded copy of *The Times*, covering up the black and white image of the Russian submarine sitting in the US Naval base.

On his bedside table, the shrill tone of the black Panasonic phone pierced the silence. The glowing orange screen revealed a +381-country code.

Serbia.

"Bloody hell." His jaw tightened. He stared at the ringing object for a moment, centering himself, before pressing the green, rubber 'talk' button. "Hello?"

The familiar, false cheeriness on the line was like papercuts in his ears. "Her Majesty's Principal Secretary of State for Defense! Please *do* remember, Johnathan, I prefer not to use my name over any electronics. Just Archer. I'm sure you remembered, though."

Johnathan's stomach sank into the bed. An unmistakable souvenir that the virtue he advertised to the world was hollow filth.

He closed his eyes. "Heya, Archer."

"I apologize for disturbing you, Johnathan. Wanted to see how you're managing with this nonsense happening in the world."

"Been a hell of a ride for sure. Our PM wants us involved up to the neck in this." He slid back into a seated position and pulled the covers over his legs.

"Well, Johnathan, I must say I'm prone to agree. If I might be so bold, I'd like to humbly ask for your help. This act by Russia is an act of war. Crew or not, in order for the sub to drift into an American harbor, they'd have to be well within the territorial seas. The US claims thirteen nautical miles from the shore. The sub would have had to be well within that range to wander into Norfolk. It's an act of war, Johnathan. An act of war."

"I'm not convinced, Archer," Johnathan replied. "I think this was a mistake. We need to deescalate tensions and let this political dust settle before we ring a bell we can *never* un-ring. A war like this would kill millions."

"Johnathan." Archer's cheery voice sharpened. "I need your help. All I'm asking is for you to suggest *strong, decisive, immediate action.* Can you *please* simply make this suggestion? I know you and I have much to share with the world. Your privacy and career are of my greatest concern. You're a dear friend, and I'd like for you to live a life without disruption. Strong, decisive, immediate action. It's all I ask, Johnathan."

"This is the extent of the favor?" The room became hot, and beads of itchy sweat bled through Jonathon's skin.

"It's all I'll ever ask. You've got my word."

His hand squeezed the phone until it shook. "I'll see what I can do in the morning."

Archer terminated the call.

Jonathon's stomach burned. There was no chance he'd sleep anytime soon. He slid the phone back into its base on his bedside table and picked up the television remote, clicking it on. Ian Bishop, a UK billionaire who spent more time with the Royal Family than anyone in Europe, stood before a sea of reporters at a press conference. Johnathan turned the volume up.

". . . and there are so many reasons we could see this as an accident. The truth is, we need to show our undaunted support for our American allies. We need to take *strong, decisive, immediate action*, and—"

With a shaking fist, Jonathon clicked off the television. "No fucking way."

"Darling?" His wife's voice echoed from the living room.

"Yep. Sorry, love. Just idiots on the TV."

He seethed, cursing Archer.

The invisible hand wrapped around his throat had more reach than he ever imagined.

CHAPTER 14

Severodvinsk, Russia

Kelly flattened herself on top of the shipping container in the dark. A large group of armed sailors crowded the area around the guards on the pier. She lifted her head an inch to see them converging on the second submarine, where Pierce was.

"Pierce, they're coming toward you. You've got about four seconds."

"Copy, I'm jumping over on the starboard side. I'll swim toward the mouth of the harbor. It's about a hundred yards. Can you get out?"

"Negative. I'm trapped. They're everywhere." The sound of Pierce hitting the water cracked into her earpiece.

A swarm of armed sailors converged on Pierce's location, barking at each other in Russian. Kelly inched backward, sliding toward the rear of the shipping container away from their view. Flakes of rusted steel crumbled under her, sending decaying metallic dust into her face. There was no chance she could walk the pier back to where they had entered. Her feet met the edge of the tall container. She continued pushing back until her legs dangled from the end. She lifted her head once more. The sailors were centrally focused on the sub. The tugboat's diesel engines roared across the harbor, no doubt heading in their direction.

She pushed the rest of her body off the container, crashing to the ground below. To her right, only ten yards away, a lone sailor hunched over a steel cleat at the edge of the pier and aimed a flashlight into the sea at the tail of the subs. Kelly drew her taser from the clipboard kit. In a crouch, she sprinted toward the sailor. Her footsteps startled him, and he spun around as Kelly leveled the stun gun. She squeezed the trigger, sending the tiny probes into the man's chest as she continued forward. His entire body stiffened and convulsed. Racing ahead without stopping, she leapt from the pier.

Kelly straightened her body and pointed her boots downward to minimize the splash. The sounds of ordinary life above water disappeared as the stabbing-cold seawater enveloped her. She popped back to the surface. To her left, the massive fins of the submarine stretched toward the sky. At sixty feet wide, the monstrous machine sat in near blackness next to an identical sister. Cylindrical fenders between the subs kept them from touching, creating several feet of space. The tugboat's engines grew louder as a white spotlight illuminated the giant black tail fin above. Kelly hauled herself back under the surface of the dark water; her muscles tightened in protest against the penetrating cold.

An almost deafening hum filled her ears. These enormous nuclear creatures generated a terror inside her, their bodily functions permeating the shallow darkness. The tugboat's spotlight searched the aft end of the sub, the white light exposing a horrifying propeller the size of a house only a few feet away from Kelly.

The narrow gap between the submarines was the darkest area Kelly could see. She focused her thoughts, dropped the clipboard into the unknown below, and slipped between the two looming, black nuclear monsters.

She fought against her heart thrashing in her chest and recalled her training at HIG.

You can last three times as long as you think you can underwater. When you think you're going to pass out, that's half of the time you can stay conscious.

Her lungs burned in protest. She dragged herself forward in the darkness, following the faint illumination of the giant silhouettes on either side of her. The shrill whine of machinery grew louder.

Kelly neared one of the fenders between the subs and forced herself to surface slowly. She hyperventilated for eight seconds to oxygenate her blood, and ducked back under the fender, continuing to pull herself along the hull in the freezing black sea.

Light breached the water's surface ahead. Kelly came up again, took another rapid series of breaths, and dove back down as deep as she could swim. She stayed along the hull of the boat and continued forward in the small shadow afforded by the sub's round design.

Kelly reached the nose of the sub and broke the surface with seconds of consciousness left. White dotted her vision. She continued forward and reached the edge of the pier. Once more, she forced herself under the surface, flirted with consciousness, and rounded the pier wall in the numbing silence. Seconds later, she finally touched sand, her vision almost black.

She crawled forward on her hands and knees, gasping for air and vomiting saltwater.

Her body was jerked violently upward. Before she knew it, she found herself laid over Pierce's shoulder, bouncing as he raced at full speed toward Viktor's pickup point.

"I'm glad you're tiny," he coughed between heaving breaths.

CHAPTER 15

Yorktown, Virginia

Deidra's heels clacked on the marble tiles as she marched down the hallway toward the HIG briefing room.

Her assistant stayed close behind, keeping pace with her clip. She entered the large conference room, where seven senior HIG officials stood upon her entry. The long room was lined with large screens and fancy leather chairs for the staff, but it had never felt so sobering. Around the mahogany table, her senior advisors stood in muted fear, their eyes narrow, faces taught.

"Please sit, everyone. Let's get updates on all fronts. Tom?" Deidra prodded.

Tom Vein, the senior intelligence officer, had worked at HIG since he had retired as the Deputy Director of the CIA. Deidra had watched him both on and off camera for three years before approaching him with the job offer. He had since proven to be one of the most valuable additions to the organization. Although he was an older man, his reverence for Deidra and the work of HIG was unmatched.

"Ma'am. We've got a new report from Norfolk. The Russian sailor they took from the sub had to be restrained. He is being held at the covert detention facility in Little Creek. At . . ." Tom lowered glasses onto his nose. ". . . 8:05 this morning, he tried to drown himself and completely lost it. They had to restrain him. His bloodwork came back with positive tests for *Toxoplasma gondii*."

Deidra took a seat at the head of the table as he spoke. "Isn't that what they found in the water supply on board the *Verkhoturye* sub in Norfolk?"

"Yes, ma'am. But now that it's in the boy's blood, they were able to isolate it. It's a hybrid strain of toxoplasma they can't identify yet. CDC is down there now, and they've been able to establish that it's some kind of hybrid parasite."

Deidra turned to Jennifer Goram, on her right. "Jennifer, you worked bio-weapons for a decade. Know anything about this?"

Jennifer, a middle-aged woman who still turned heads, leaned forward and rested her elbows on the table, her fingers steepled. "Toxoplasma is a protozoan parasite. A single-celled organism. It can infect any mammal but can only sexually reproduce in cats. When humans get infected, it targets the brain directly. Studies suggest that it's directly tied to schizophrenia and bipolar disorders, but it's not conclusive as far as I remember."

Deidra scribbled a note in her notebook. "Okay. So, is it a bioweapon? Can it be manufactured to do this?"

Jennifer shook her head. "I've never heard of it. I called several people I'm connected with at the CDC and Army Weapons Lab. They all say it can't be weaponized as far as they know."

"Toxoplasma only targets the brains of humans?" Deidra asked.

"No. Almost any warm-blooded animal. Since the parasite reproduces in cats, it has evolved to control the minds of rats. If a rat is exposed to it, it makes the rat seek out the smell of cat urine. Most rats stay away from anything that smells like cats, but when they get toxoplasma, they become obsessed with it. This makes them more likely to be eaten by the cats, where the toxoplasma can reproduce."

Tom pulled off his glasses. "My god. That's real?"

"Yes. It's gross, but it's proven science."

The staff in the room tried to conceal their stunned expressions. Their eyebrows rose almost in unison.

Jennifer put up a hand. "It's not proven to control *human* minds. It's not possible from what

I've learned. What we got off the *Verkhoturye* was *Toxoplasma gondii*, but it was modified. We're waiting on results."

Leaning back in her chair, Deidra clasped her hands in her lap. If this escalated, her options would be limited. She wished Alex Frost were still around. Her stomach tightened as she made her announcement.

"For now, we will treat this as a bioweapon. Initiate protocols for bioweapon containment. If this is on one Russian sub, it's probably on more. We need to find out. Get the samples from Pierce ASAP." She aimed a pointed look at Tom. "What's with the routing number Pierce found in the apartment?"

Tom slipped a page from the leather folio on the table before him.

"It's what's called an IBAN. International Bank Account Number. We traced it back to a shell company in Belgrade. The company is owned by a private trust based here in the US. In Wyoming. We discovered early this morning that the account has been paying the two Serbian shipyard workers for almost a year. Both of them had access to the *Verkhoturye*—I have no doubt they are behind this. The local police found them both dead in their beds, and they both had intricate drawings of submarine water supply systems in their apartments."

Deidra processed this new information. "Is this why the Russian Navy has pulled all their subs back to port?"

"The subs can't depart the port because Russian sailors have started testing positive for radiation exposure. The Russians recalled the submarines; they think there could be a faulty shielding mechanism. The sailors who tested positive were crew members on several different submarines. It crippled their Navy. They can't deploy the subs until they find the source of the radiation. Our people in Russia say there have been zero indications of radioactivity leakage on the submarines."

The room was silent. The expectancy of her colleagues sent a solemn chill through her chest. Deidra swallowed and sat upright. "Send Pierce and Kelly to Belgrade. And get me their samples. We may only have a few hours to get this figured out before some dipshit launches a missile."

CHAPTER 16

Severodvinsk, Russia

Fyodor nudged his delivery truck into its parking place in the Russian Naval Barracks and prepared for the final night of his operation. The three four-story buildings around him full of sleeping Russian sailors would soon be only a memory. Two weeks of parking in this same spot for hours had been easy enough, but his concern wasn't for the banality of the operation. It was for the machine bolted into the cargo space behind him.

A long overdue vacation lay promptly ahead. A fortune greater than he'd seen in his lifetime awaited him after this final night of work.

Mounted to the inside wall of the cargo bay was a Bhabhatron. A radiation therapy machine converted to fit inside the truck. Inside the machine, the radioactive element cobalt-60 was used to treat cancer a decade earlier in Moscow.

Now, however, it was modified into a venomous monster.

Fyodor was no expert. The masked men who delivered the truck had showed him a small compartment called the 'PIG.' They told him never to open it. And he didn't.

The men had carefully rigged a long, thick cable from the machine into the cab of the truck. At the end of this cable, they attached a small grey box for him, housing a switch and a dial. The switch turned the machine on, and the dial adjusted the aperture of the radiation device from one millimeter to twenty centimeters.

His task was a simple one: keep the side of the van pointed at one building for thirty-five minutes, change directions to the next building for the same amount of time, and repeat for the third.

The other job they paid him to do was completed. They told him to park outside two other apartment buildings in the city and aim the device upward at a specific apartment for several hours in the night, with a focused aperture of fourteen centimeters. Earlier this morning, he read about the two men in the paper and hoped that he, too, would die in his sleep someday, far in the future. His work was noble, dangerous, and fortuitous to his family.

Fyodor reached beside him and dragged a heavy lead blanket over himself as he did each evening. Once nestled inside, he reached out of the blanket and flipped the switch on the small, grey, plastic box beside him. As he was trained, he counted to five and gradually rotated the dial, adjusting the aperture setting to twenty centimeters. The machine behind him hummed to life, and Fyodor tucked into his warm, protective blanket for his final night of work. Tomorrow, he would be a rich man.

CHAPTER 17

Severodvinsk, Russia

"We've used Markov chain Monte Carlo sampling and PCR. Toxoplasma was rampant in the water supply of the sub here in Norfolk," Jason Mittenberg, a trusted HIG asset who specialized in microbiology and chemical compounds, said through Pierce's speaker phone.

"Jason, first, I don't know what the hell Markov Chevy Monte-Carlo is. Second, toxoplasma sounds like something from *Star Trek*. Let's keep this on a second-grade level for me here."

The van slipped through the night; the headlights illuminated the decaying apartment buildings in the west end of the city. Pierce, soaking wet and covered in sand, buried his face in his hand.

"Yes, sir. Sorry, Mister Reston. We tested the water a second time from the sub. The samples

Kelly got from the sink in Norfolk. There is a parasite in there that targets the brain but it has been modified."

Kelly sat next to Pierce in the back seat of Viktor's van, curled into a shivering ball, her wet hair peppered with sand.

"Like, modified by years of evolution, or modified by some nerd in a lab?"

"Most likely the nerd scenario, sir. We need the samples you got from the sub there within the hour to make sure this is something we can let the Russians know. If this is in the water supply of more of their ships, we're going to have a major issue. Nuclear—"

"Got it. How are we getting these to you, Jason? FedEx?"

Jason chuckled, but Pierce wasn't joking. The young man cleared his throat. "Uh, no. I'm having a local come to you to get them. He's a university researcher and we've used him once before in 2012 with the chemical stuff from Syria."

"Roger. Thanks. What's PCR?"

"Sorry. Yes. Polymerase chain reaction. It's a fancy test for toxoplasma. The contact we set up for you is a researcher at Arkhangel'skiy Meditsinskiy Kolledzh. It's' a local medical school. Can you send me your location?"

"Copy. We're about to stop at the Scout's house now." Pierce tapped his phone screen. "Location sent."

He ended the call as Viktor eased the van into his driveway. Kelly placed a shivering hand on the door handle and stumbled into the driveway. The group walked the narrow sidewalk to Viktor's rundown house.

"Nice place, Viktor," Kelly said.

"Thank you. Your company pays me very good."

Viktor swung open his front door to reveal a miniscule living room. Pierce eyed the fading white paint on the walls. A lone couch was positioned against the wall in front of a television. A coffee table sat before the sofa, topped with a pizza box and a Play Station controller.

"Viktor, I need to get some clothes," Kelly managed.

"Yes. I think there is probably nothing open at this time in the night. Maybe I can give you something?"

"That would be great. Thank you."

"Okay—Mister Pierce? You need shirt or something?"

"Thanks, Viktor. I'm good. I have another set here in the bag. Kelly didn't pack well."

Kelly shot a glare back at Pierce.

"No problem, you guys. Please wait one minute." Viktor trotted down the narrow hallway.

Kelly slid the back door open to a small, dark patio and shook sand out of her wet clothes and hair. She yanked at the zipper of the coveralls and stripped them off, revealing dark slacks and a white blouse.

"That's some James Bond stuff right there, Kell."

"More like *Naked and Afraid* right now." Pierce laughed. Kelly kicked off her small boots and peeled the wet slacks off her legs. She wrestled with her blouse for a moment and tossed it into a heap of damp, sandy clothing on Viktor's patio. "It's warmer out here." With a smile, she leaned forward and shook the sand from her hair, her underwear clinging to her body.

Viktor appeared in the hallway, proudly carrying a rolled-up outfit he'd selected for Kelly. He saw her standing in her underwear and turned away. He stretched his arm backward to Kelly with the clothes.

Kelly didn't flinch. She stepped in and took the clothing from Viktor's outstretched hand. "I'm going to shower real quick if that's okay."

"Yes. Yes. There." Viktor pointed to the hallway. "Door on left." He continued nervously shielding his eyes. Pierce wondered whether Viktor did this out of courtesy or because he knew she was a trained killer. Either way, it was a nice gesture.

Kelly shut the bathroom door, and Pierce's phone buzzed.

"Mister Reston? Our laboratory man is outside. He's in a white Lada Niva SUV."

"Thanks. Name?"

"He goes by Dima."

Pierce ended the call, retrieved a Glock from his black sling bag, and tucked it into the cargo pocket of the coveralls. Grabbing the now dented clipboard, he walked out to the end of the driveway, where a man sat waiting in an SUV. He handed the clipboard through the window.

"Hello, sir."

"Hi, Dima. This should be all you need."

Dima flipped the latch on the clipboard and recoiled as droplets of seawater and sand spilled into his lap.

"You can keep the taser. A gift from me."

"Oh. Uh. Yes. Very kind." Dima nodded with a nervous smile and slid the clipboard between the passenger seat and the center console. "I will have test result sent to the email they give me on phone?"

"That's fine. Thank you."

Pierce waved and walked back into the house. After a cup of bitter Russian coffee, Pierce and Viktor turned as Kelly emerged from the hallway.

Kelly made her way into the kitchen wearing the outfit Viktor had chosen for her, still drying her shoulder-length hair with a towel. Pierce struggled to contain himself. Kelly stood, expressionless, allowing them both to take it in.

Around her petite waist, she wore a set of faded blue Adidas running shorts that were cinched so tight the strings dangled. The worn-out, white t-shirt Viktor had chosen featured a large image of Cuba. When Pierce read the three words printed underneath, he could no longer hold back.

Havana Good Time!

*****

Pierce's iPad screen flashed to life on the kitchen table. He swiped it open. Kelly came to the table and rested a hand on the back of his chair.

"HIG delivered a new mission package. We need to get to Belgrade." He clicked on an embedded map image. "Looks like whoever is behind this is running the show from Belgrade. The two guys who died, the money—there's a virologist there who agreed to meet with us through an asset. We have to meet with him in six hours."

Kelly glanced at her watch. "How far is Belgrade? A thousand miles?"

"Yeah. Probably. Viktor, I'm going to get a quick shower as well if you don't mind."

"Please. Yes. It's okay." Viktor gestured back to the hall.

"Thanks. I'll be right out. Kelly, call and get the plane ready."

CHAPTER 18

Washington, DC

Vincent Braid dragged off his tie, rolled it around his hand, and slid it into the pocket of his slacks. He pulled open the door of his home at the Naval Observatory. His slow steps echoed off the hardwood floors. He would normally relish these few days when his wife left on the literacy tours across the country; the time alone offered him mental space to decompress and think through current events with an ice-cold beer in hand.

Not today, though. He'd been in two interviews and the relentless media pressured him to take a firm stance for or against action. For some reason, he had refused to commit. The Archer had never asked anything of him until this morning. And he'd never known the man's reach until he'd seen a dozen of his close friends use the phrase he'd been told to regurgitate into soulless camera lenses.

Strong, decisive, immediate action. Why the hell would this matter to an investment banker like the Archer?

Vincent yanked open the refrigerator and grabbed a bottle of Bud Light. He plodded to the wood-paneled study, dropped into a leather armchair, and tossed the beer cap onto the oak coffee table in front of him.

The Archer had never requested anything of him. However, he was the reason Vincent had won the election. The man's connections were endless.

His thoughts drifted back to the moment he'd first regretted meeting with the man.

A few years prior, he had stepped aboard Miss Tart, Archer's behemoth yacht in Port Hercule, Monte Carlo. Within hours, he had ingested more than a reasonable amount of champagne and agreed to borrow a pair of swim trunks from the Archer. Not long after, Vincent found himself in a hot tub with him and two young women whom the Archer introduced as hospitality interns from Serbia. The young girls' smooth skin, soft hair, and bright complexions made them look incredibly young. Vincent assumed it was Serbian genetics.

Three glasses of champagne later, he found himself on a private massage table. One of the young woman's hands between his legs.

This continued in his private stateroom, and he made the mistake a few more times before the boat returned to the harbor three days later.

The Archer and his security escorted Vincent to his car on the pier and handed over a gift basket of scotch, whiskey, and glasses emblazoned with the Archer's company seal.

As the Archer walked him across the brow to the pier, he put a hand on Vincent's shoulder. "Vincent, I know security is huge for you. I want to assure you that I'm your friend. You don't have to worry about anything. It all stays on the boat. I do have security cameras throughout the entire boat, but I can assure you that it's kept secure. Not even your own NSA could access the files. You have absolutely nothing to worry about."

Vincent's stomach sank. At a loss for words, he defaulted to the political mask he'd been fabricating for the past three decades. He concealed the anger, fear, and regret, and thanked his new friend for the trip before climbing into a white Mercedes to the airport.

"Sir? You need anything?" Vincent's Secret Service man's voice brought him back into the study. The cold beer had dripped condensation down the arm of the leather chair.

"No. Thanks, Jim. I'm fine for the rest of the day."

"Yes, sir. We'll be outside."

Vincent stared out the window at the domed observatory across the circle.

What is the cost of inaction?

CHAPTER 19

GeopoliticalTimes.com

BREAKING NEWS

DESPITE TENSIONS, RUSSIAN SUBS STUCK AT HOME

Moscow has escalated tensions amidst the recent developments in Norfolk, Virginia, dispatching their naval fleet to America's Eastern seaboard.

Despite the escalation, however, Russian submarines have been mysteriously on house arrest in Severodvinsk. Even submarines that were out to sea have been recalled to base.

Rumors are circulating after a video surfaced showing what experts believe are Russian sailors undergoing radiation sickness treatment. The more prominent rumors are that a potential nuclear leak at the naval base has caused an emergency recall of the submarines.

We will keep you updated on all the latest news.

CHAPTER 20

Belgrade, Serbia

Pierce received the update just before takeoff: more toxoplasma in the water supply. Their new mission was to track down the financial origin of the operation. A shell company in Belgrade, Serbia that had several ties to microbiology research companies.

Mariel had arranged a meeting for them in a few hours. A local infectious disease expert had agreed to meet them at 3:30 AM in Belgrade.

"How are we supposed to figure out what's going on before the Russian fleet arrives in the US?" Kelly asked. She continued shuffling through the stack of papers as the engines roared.

The plane touched down at Nikola Tesla Airport at 2:25 AM. Kelly had changed into khaki pants and a slim-fitting button-down shirt. Pierce wore stretchy slacks and a suit tailored to conceal his pistol.

"We've got thirty-five minutes to get to the contact. He wants to meet at a Mitsubishi dealership for some reason."

"It's three in the morning," Kelly said. The plane steered to the right, toward a private hangar at the southeast end of the airport. To Pierce's left, dismembered bodies of planes sat in a scrap yard beside the hangar.

"I know. It's near his home, and he can't meet us in his laboratory."

In the hangar, the pilots cranked open the door and lowered the stairs to a polished concrete floor. Three customs officials stood at the base of the stairs. Pierce and Kelly handed over their black Diplomatic passports to the officials, and they were politely welcomed to Serbia.

Their local Scout stood next to a Ford Expedition wearing a perfectly cut suit and tie. The Scout's fake US Embassy credentials hung from a green lanyard around his neck. The tall, slim man trotted over to them as the customs officials climbed into a golf cart and departed the hangar.

"Hello. I'm Emir. I have been working for your company for maybe, like, five years. Very good people."

"Thanks, Emir. I'm glad they take good care of you. The password is Viking, Rhino, Six."

The Scout's face softened. Kelly looked amused at seeing the transition to 'Scout Mode.'

The three exchanged pleasantries and Emir clicked on his cell phone. "I think we can be at the location in about forty minutes if we take the A3. You're still going to Velauto Plus on Vojvode Stepe, correct?"

Pierce nodded. Kelly began throwing their bags into the rear of the vehicle. "Is there anything special about this location, Emir?"

"No, ma'am. I think nothing is very special here. It is closed for sure—nighttime."

On the half-hour drive, Emir talked about his affection for chess-playing and his ambitions to win the upcoming world-famous Tata Steel chess championship. "Chess, for me, is an amazing feeling. To win the game, it's a feeling that is hard to describe." A misty rain made the highway reflective.

Pierce made mental notes on the Scout's behavioral profile, the adjectives he'd chosen, and his use of the word *feeling*, revealing the sensory words he was likely to respond to. He continued flicking through the images of the meeting area with Kelly. If their local contact had set up a kill box, he'd likely use a less public place. But at three in the morning, it wouldn't be hard to fire a silenced weapon in the streets of Belgrade. There were three places a sniper could be positioned around the Mitsubishi dealer.

They rehearsed their plans for the meeting two more times, including the three fallback plans. Emir navigated through city streets in the rain and came to a stop next to the smallest gas station Pierce had ever seen, simply labeled 'Sponit.' Two pumps bordered what was essentially a sidewalk beside the road.

"You need gas, Emir?"

Emir twisted around and shook his head. "Oh. No. No. I know when your people visit here, they never like to go exactly to the location. You want me to drive all the way, it's only two hundred meters up around this corner." Emir motioned to a hard left turn in the road just ahead through the rain.

"Let's walk it," Kelly said.

Pierce nodded in agreement. "The rain isn't too bad." He passed a phone to Emir. "I'm going to keep a call active during the meeting so you can be ready if anything happens."

The phone trilled, and Emir placed it on speaker and set it on the dashboard beside a figurine of a large rook chess piece.

They loaded their pistols into concealed Kydex holsters and hopped out of the back seat of the SUV. Pierce tilted his head back and closed his eyes, allowing the cool, misty rain to fall onto his face. They followed the curve in the road. Short apartment buildings and small houses along the sides of the street sat in silence. The streetlights offered a muted, occasional glow to the road. The dark Mitsubishi dealership sat only a hundred yards ahead. As they neared the building, an older man holding a black umbrella emerged from a shadow. He waved them over.

"His arms are relaxed. He's not scanning. Looks like he's alone," Kelly said.

"Agreed. Nice job."

Kelly grinned.

"Hello! I'm Doctor Konikoff," the old man said. He stood dressed in striped pajamas under his umbrella, extending a hand.

"Hi, Doctor," Pierce said, taking his hand. "Thanks for agreeing to meet with us. This is Nancy Bridges. I'm Peter Vick."

"Of course. What do you need from me? Is this about the submarine thing in America? I hear your accents now." The doctor stepped forward to hold part of his umbrella over Kelly.

"It is. We don't think it was Russian involvement at all."

"I guessed that myself when I heard the sailors were all missing," Konikoff responded.

Pierce stepped under a small overhang at the side of the Mitsubishi dealership while Kelly scanned for unusual activity around them.

"Well, they aren't all missing. There was one sailor who was still on board."

The doctor's eyes widened. "Oh? That sounds like a valuable source for information. I'm guessing since you've asked for my help, you think there is some biological weapon involved here? I must tell you, I don't give a crap about the political landscape. Science holds our countries together. That's why the Russians and Americans coexist in space exploration. The scientists are smarter than the politicians."

"Doctor, I assure you we are interested in the same thing. We've spent a lifetime talking naive politicians out of making stupid decisions. We're concerned about peace. *Only* peace."

A man in a transparent poncho buzzed past them on a moped, groceries dangling from the handlebars. The doctor looked at the ground for a moment in silence, then eyed Kelly with skepticism, noticing her surveying the area around them. "What agency are you? CIA?"

"No. State Department."

"Ah. I see." The doctor motioned quotations in the air with his free hand. "'State Department.' Well, what can I do?"

"You're one of the leading researchers in the field, and the Americans can't figure out what's going on. Samples from the Russian submarine showed we had high levels of toxoplasma in the water. The Russian sailor we took from the sub is now in hospital. He was trying to drown himself. He said the others abandoned ship. Jumped into the ocean." Pierce shook his head.

"*Toxoplasma gondii*?" The doctor gazed at the street, scratching his face.

"Yes. Sorry."

The man shook his head, his eyes far away. Pierce didn't disturb him. His wrinkled face and fragile features seemed to shrink. "I'm certain there is no way *Toxoplasma gondii* could cause that reaction. It can make people act crazy because it targets the brain, but there's no way—" he stopped, silent once more—rubbing his face. "This sailor says they jumped in the ocean *willingly*—knowing they would die?"

"That's what he told the US Navy personnel who rescued him, yes." Pierce adjusted his collar against the rain and scanned the windows around them.

A buzzing motorcycle engine roared to life in the distance.

After a moment of silence, Konikoff looked up again to Kelly, then to Pierce. "Like the crickets! It's the same as a cricket."

Pierce and Kelly exchanged confused glances. "What crickets, Doctor?" Kelly pushed a cluster of wet hair from her face and tucked it behind her ear.

The doctor straightened. "Crickets do the same. Look! Do you see these?" He motioned to a puddle beside Kelly's feet.

Pierce looked down at the puddle as the sound of the motorcycle neared. There was nothing remarkable in the puddle. It looked like a puddle of rain in the street—like any other puddle he'd seen in his life. "Doctor, I don't really see anythi—"

Two muffled cracks echoed in the street behind them. The doctor stumbled backward. Pierce spun in a crouch, drawing his pistol to see a person dressed in black speeding off on a motorcycle.

*****

Pierce hadn't realized it, but he'd pulled Kelly down to the ground when he heard the sounds. He shot up into a crouch and seized her shoulders, searching through the folds of her clothing for gunshot wounds.

Kelly rolled away and stood on her own, searching the street for the shooter. "I'm fine. Was that—?"

Pierce knew the sound well—a silenced pistol. He looked back to the doctor, now motionless on the ground. His umbrella hobbled away with the breeze. Dark blood soaked through two holes in the man's chest into the surrounding fabric of his pajamas, which spread quickly in the falling mist.

Kelly knelt and pressed her fingers to the man's neck. "He's dead. I think one hit his heart."

"Jesus. We can't leave him here. We need to hide him until we get to the bottom of this Russian shit. Grab his feet." Pierce angled his mouth to the phone in his breast pocket. "Emir, get down here now!"

Kelly gripped the man's ankles. Pierce hooked his hands under the armpits.

"There's a green area to the left of the dealership. We can put him in the grass. It'll be a day or so before someone finds him."

Listening intently for vehicles, they hauled the body to a small grassy area just to the left of the tiny Mitsubishi dealership. Kelly let his feet slide down into a deep area of tall, wet grass, and Pierce lowered his torso. Even standing beside the body, the doctor was almost invisible. The rain would hopefully conceal him for a time, reducing the foot traffic in the vicinity.

Tires skidded in the street beside them. Emir leapt from the SUV and came around the hood to the sidewalk. "All good here?"

"The doctor's dead. Someone drove by and shot him," Kelly announced, searching the street again.

"Yes. I heard it on the phone. A motorcycle." Emir handed a folded green towel to Kelly. Kelly took it and wiped a streak of blood from her fingers. "Let's get the hell out of here."

Pierce dialed HIG as they climbed into the rear of the SUV.

"Hey, Pierce." Mariel's steady voice came through the speaker. No matter what kind of trouble he was in, her calm was always contagious.

"We met with the local source here. I have you on speaker. The asset is with us now. The source was shot by someone on a motorcycle. Five-eight, a hundred seventy pounds, most likely male."

"Copy. Is the source dead?"

"Yeah. Before it happened, he mentioned crickets and pointed to a puddle in the street. He said toxoplasma can't be responsible for this, but then he got enthusiastic when he mentioned puddles and crickets."

"Crickets? Like the insect, right?"

"Yeah."

"Is that all he said?"

"When we told him the sailors allegedly jumped off the sub to their death, he said crickets do the same, then he pointed to the puddle—he was *really* excited about the puddle."

"What's with the puddle?" Mariel asked.

"I have no idea. It was a normal puddle."

"Hold on. I'm getting our expert on the line now. Stand by, Pierce."

Emir sped through the wet streets until he found an unlit parking garage a minute away. He rolled down a steep ramp into the structure and parked the SUV.

A beep shot from the phone speaker and a man's voice came onto the line. "Hello?"

"Doctor Wilson, please meet Pierce Reston. He just met with an expert and we're having trouble making sense of what he's told us."

"Okay. Hello, Pierce. Good to meet you. You'll have to excuse the noise—my kids are getting ready for bed here."

"Thanks, Doctor Wilson. So, as of now, we asked our expert here about the toxoplasma stuff. He tells us that there's *no* way toxoplasma could cause what happened with the submarine—people jumping off."

"I agree with that, Pierce. That's not possible. We're running tests right now to see if there's something we missed."

"Okay. Well, the doctor here in Serbia started talking about crickets. He got really excited and talked about how crickets do that too and pointed to a puddle."

"Like—a puddle of crickets?" Dr. Wilson asked.

Pierce reiterated that it was a regular rain puddle.

"Strange. Alright. Was there anything different about this puddle?"

Kelly shot a hand into the air and tilted toward the phone. "Hey, Doc. Kelly Kennedy here. There *were* little worm things. Like those wiggly, skinny worms that you see in almost every rain puddle in

America. But nothing else. We thought he was trying to tell us about rainwater pollution or something."

The HIG doctor's voice quieted. "Hold on, guys." The sound of a keyboard clicking in the background came through the speaker. Then silence. After a moment, the doctor came back. "My God! That doctor got excited because he identified a similar pattern. Those little worms are called hairworms. They are parasites, but they contain something called effector molecules."

Emir turned right down a dark road. Pierce and Kelly exchanged glances as the doctor continued.

"They come into contact with a cricket and invade the cricket's body. They literally control the cricket's mind and make it commit suicide by jumping into water. The worms then breed inside the cricket's body and hatch out of it into the water. They even control the cricket by keeping it from chirping. If the cricket chirps, it's more likely to be eaten by predators, so the worm turns off the desire to make those little cricket sounds."

Kelly grimaced. "That's horrifying. So, Doctor, do you think this is what we're dealing with?"

"It could be. We're going to run a few tests specifically for this. I'm reading through some papers on it now. It's called *Spinochordodes tellinii*. If that's been spliced somehow with toxoplasma, it would target the human brain, for sure. There's no possible way of knowing what it's capable of doing."

Pierce pushed his wet hair to the side. "I've been doing this for a long time, and I've never heard of mind control *worms.*"

After a pause, the doctor replied in a grave, hushed voice, "If this is in other ships, we're in big trouble."

CHAPTER 21

Washington, DC

Vincent Braid stood alone in his kitchen re-reading the latest text message from Archer.

> *'I know you're under a lot of stress, but I failed to see your help today in the media. We each honor our friendship by helping the other. I agreed I would always hold your secrets in the strictest of confidence. I've never asked for anything before, and I'd like to honor my side of our friendship . . . YOU DESERVE PRIVACY.'*

Provoking a war with Russia would be catastrophic. There was enough inflammatory bullshit on the media. He could easily convince the president to take action—he had served as the silent advisor to him for years before the election, and well into the presidency.

Vincent flicked on the small television on the kitchen counter and tapped the remote. Fox News was mid-interview with Brooke Thompson, who had just been appointed to the position of Secretary of the Navy following extensive Senate confirmation hearings. Her dark suit and pearls looked like funeral attire.

The vice president unmuted the television.

". . . going to be a disaster. The Russians have deliberately violated international law. Empty or not, this submarine shows us they are operating in our twelve-mile territorial waters. Although we've offered to cooperate with Russia, they are responding to our offer by dispatching a fleet to American shores. Russia's actions speak for themselves. If this isn't a clear-cut act of war, I don't know what is. Our citizens, our military, and our entire way of life is at grave risk. We need to take *strong, decisive, immediate action* to stop this before it escalates to a point of no return."

"Thank you, Madam Secretary. Coming up nex—"

Vincent mashed the mute button again. The words that exited the secretary's mouth made his skin crawl. He'd never seen her with The Archer before. This had to stop.

Tomorrow evening, the Russian fleet will be dotting the horizon of our Eastern shores.

He slid his private phone toward him on the counter, opened the contacts, and typed 'R.'

A name he prayed he would never have to call materialized on the screen. He reached forward and hesitated, his hand hovering over the call button.

He closed his eyes and pressed it.

The phone began ringing, and the man's name appeared in bold letters at the top of the vice president's screen.

Pierce Reston.

CHAPTER 22

Moscow, Russia

Admiral Dimitri Kostyukov pushed back from his desk as one of his officers updated him on the latest intelligence. The officer stood before his desk, hands clasped together in submission as he spoke. Dimitri fiddled with silver pen as he listened.

"Sir, we traced the two Serbians back to their previous employment in Belgrade. Both were getting money from a ghost account in Serbia. They provided false documents one year ago and have since worked on thirty-eight ships and submarines."

The young officer cleared his throat and continued, "If what the Americans are saying is true, it could be a form of biological weapon. None of the submarines are testing positive for nuclear shielding failures or leaks. We cannot find the source of the radiation, but the detectors set up in

Severodvinsk have detected *neutron* radiation—it didn't come from our submarines, sir."

The admiral sat forward and stared at a printed photo of the two men on his desk, taken in Belgrade as they applied to work in the shipyard. "What is in Belgrade? An account alone or something else?"

The officer leafed through a stack of papers in a folder and withdrew a yellow paper with '***секрет***' written across the top and bottom. "Sir, we traced the men's online communications to a company owned by an American who owns a vacation home in Belgrade."

The admiral slammed his palm onto the desk, making the younger officer take a step back.

"These damn Americans. I'm telling you now, Lieutenant, *this* is a scam. They will pay for this. We're going to Belgrade. Sounds like CIA to me. I'm going to make a few calls now. We need to take a strong stance against the Americans, and if this man is involved, I want the FSB there with me to put his head on a spike. We can show the world that the Americans were behind this. How many FSB officers do we have in Belgrade?"

The officer shook his head. "I don't know, Admiral Kostyukov. At least five."

The admiral stood with clamped fists. "Tell the fleet to come up to full speed to Norfolk. Get me a plane ready for Belgrade now and have the local FSB meet me at the airport."

CHAPTER 23

Belgrade, Serbia

"I snatched the cell phone off the dead guy." Kelly wiped the rain from her face and blotted the phone with the green towel Emir had kindly offered earlier.

Emir continued driving on the narrow road past a small, abandoned shopping center.

"Wow. Nice. Is it locked with a passcode?" Pierce eyed the device in her hand.

She eyed Pierce with a clever grin. "It did." Kelly swiped a finger up the screen and the phone unlocked. "I used his thumb to unlock it and turn off the security."

"Emir, let's stay near this area for a minute until we figure this out."

Emir nodded. "We're still very close. I've not gone far."

Pierce leaned into Kelly, who was already scrolling through messages.

Emir turned into a bank parking lot and shifted into park. "Of course, no problem."

Kelly searched the phone for keywords—'toxoplasma,' 'crickets,' 'cats,' 'hairworm.' The hairworm search turned up three results. Two research papers from 1993, and one reminder. She tapped on a reminder marked as completed.

Send hairworm data to Nils

"Who's Nils?" Kelly asked.

"No clue. Lemme check." Pierce withdrew his iPad and typed several terms into a search bar.

The third search result led him to a Nobel Prize recipient's dinner reception page. A scientist named Nils Camus had received a Nobel Prize for something called 'osmolality modulation in common parasites.'

He searched again for the man's name and discovered he lived in Belgrade and was a researcher at the Torlak Institute of Virology only minutes away.

Kelly jabbed a finger at the iPad. "Type in his name with Belgrade after it."

The first result was a news article published the previous evening.

Politika Ekspress

FAMED SCIENTIST AND RESEARCHER REPORTED MISSING

Nobel Prize recipient Nils Camus is known for his work in developing and compounding organisms. His Nobel Prize was awarded for work in developing a parasite that could be ingested to keep bacteria from infecting villagers in Eastern Africa. Doctor Camus has been missing for three days now. If you have any information about his whereabouts, please contact the local police immediately at 011192.

"Well, that's interesting." Kelly sat back in her seat and searched on her phone for 'Torlak Institute of Virology.' A result popped up with a location labeled 'Институт за вирусологију, вакцине и серуме Торлак.' Kelly stretched her phone forward to Emir. "Is this it?"

Emir twisted around in the front seat and mouthed the words as he read. "Yes. That's what it says. Only few minutes from here." He gestured out the windshield.

Pierce rifled through the sling bag at his feet and brought up a small pouch. He opened it and withdrew a World Health Organization identification card. "If this guy was involved at all, we need to get inside this lab. Emir, let's get to there. Kelly and I are breaking in."

*****

Pierce's phone buzzed in his hand as Emir drove toward the lab only minutes away. The small screen painted the back seat in soft white light. He glanced down, seeing an incoming call. "Well, this should be interesting."

Kelly leaned over and stared at the phone; her mouth dropped. "You know the *vice president*?"

Pierce shook his head. "Not really. We've only met a few times. There are people in the government who know we exist. Vince is one of them." Pierce released a sigh and slid the button on his screen to the right.

"Hey, Vince."

After a brief silence, the familiar voice came through the speaker. "Pierce?"

"Yes, sir. It's me. What's going on?" Pierce replied.

"Yes. Yes. I wanted to see what all is happening on your end. Anything new?"

"Well, yes. We've found the source of the missing sailors, as far as I can tell. Looks like something called . . ." Pierce glanced back at his iPad to make sure he pronounced it correctly. ". . . toxoplasma gondii."

"I've heard about the toxoplasma. Our experts are saying it's not possible for it to cause something like this."

Pierce scrolled down the screen a bit further. "It's toxoplasma, but it was mixed with something called hairworm. It's a parasite that makes crickets jump into water and commit suicide. We're tracking it down in Belgrade now."

The vice president's voice shook. "Belgrade?"

"Yeah. We think one of the locals here may have been involved. Name is Nils Camus. But he went missing a couple days ago. He's some kind of researcher."

"I know Nils. Well—I don't *know* him. I've met him at a few dinners. We have mutual friends. He does research into water treatment or something like that."

Pierce raised an eyebrow. "Vince, did you guys have anyone in particular that maybe all your other mutual friends also had in common? It's looking like this thing is originating in Belgrade. Both chemically and financially."

The vice president exhaled an almost inaudible, "Fuck."

Kelly's mouth hung open, laser-focused on the phone. She rotated her hand in the air, silently urging the vice president to continue. He let out a long breath.

"Pierce. You guys could basically talk me into anything right?"

"Vince, you know we have protocols for th—"

"I mean you're capable of it though, right?"

"Sure. I could make you deliver a press conference naked if I wanted. Yes."

The vice president sighed again. "I've made some mistakes. I'm not perfect. I have no idea what's coming in the next few hours, so I have to prioritize the country over myself." Braid paused; his deep breathing audible through the speaker. After a moment, Braid exhaled and continued, "Over the previous few years, I've made some pretty bad mistakes. They may be used against me—the mistakes have made me beholden to someone who can expose everything. I've *got* to side with our country."

"Vince, what's going on?"

"I—I know who might be the mutual friend that all the mutual friends have in common. Nils has been with me on the boat before, after he won the Nobel Prize. Pierce, I don't know how to say this. I'm not capitulating to this monster. Tomorrow I may be destroyed because of it. I'll be impeached immediately."

Pierce worried the man may decide not to share anything and prepared to launch into Phrase One through the phone. Nobody would blame him if he used Tradecraft in a situation like this.

The vice president cleared his throat and began speaking again. "There were...underage girls. Russians or something. And everything happened so fast."

Pierce ran his hand through his hair and sat back into the seat. He didn't have time to go through the motions. He knew the vice president was on the verge of coughing it all up, probably due to the innate human need to confess, but Pierce didn't have time. "Vince, I need the name."

"Right. Yes. I'm not sure he's behind this, but he's been pushing me to make this into a war. Wants me to get the military to take action. I think he's doing something behind the scenes with all this."

Emir rounded a corner and an unlit, narrow, street lined with tall trees appeared ahead of them. His eyes were wide in the rearview mirror as he listened to the call in his back seat.

"Vince, you did the right thing here. You have held the office in the highest regard, and you placed the country's needs above your own. I just need the name." Pierce didn't use interrogation techniques often, but he needed the information whether or not it protected Vince's ego.

"E-Ethan Peterson. But he won't let anyone use his name over phones and such. He wants everyone to call him The Archer.

Pierce and Kelly squinted at each other.

"The business guy? Billionaire?"

"Y-Yes. He called me from Belgrade earlier tonight. He has a house there directly across the street from the US Embassy on Solina."

"And you and he are friends?"

"That's a stretch. He's made a pyramid scheme out of politicians his whole life. He will give you more campaign contributions the more people you introduce him to. He works the same way with the girls he brings in. For every young girl, they get paid fifteen percent more for each younger girl they can recruit and bring in. They are showing up at that house night and day. He called me earlier and asked me to make statements to the press that I think will push us closer to war with Russia. I need to make this right."

Emir, who until now had been silent in the driver's seat, twisted around to Pierce and Kelly. "He's playing chess with humans," he whispered.

Emir was right. Pierce focused back on his phone. "Vince, he may be puppeteering some of this, but do you think he's involved?"

"He's never asked me for anything before. This is highly unusual. This must be something huge for him. He could certainly afford to orchestrate this kind of thing."

"Thanks, Vince. We're heading to a lab to get our samples. I'll update HIG. We'll head to his house after and pay him a visit."

"Pierce, thank you. Please be careful. If you're not a sixteen-year-old girl, the security guys will be on alert. I hope I helped. I can't push our country into a war."

"Sir, you've been more than a help. Thank you. You did the right thing for the country. In Washington, DC, patriotism is the rarest quality to have. You people eat your young."

Pierce ended the call.

Kelly tucked her hair behind her ears and shook her head. "Disgusting. But I'm glad we got some intel. Never thought I'd be hearing the vice president's voice like that. He's *terrified*."

"Indeed. Emir, let's get to that lab while we still have darkness on our side." He focused on Kelly's eyes. "We're going to need to get you some new clothes. Think you can pass for a teenager?"

CHAPTER 24

Washington, DC

Vincent walked through his kitchen into the foyer. He lifted a windbreaker from a brass hook and slowly put it on. In the hundred-year-old table in front of him, Vince found the handle for the middle drawer and slid it open. The heavy drawer slid forward, revealing an empty space, save for a single item. A green stretchy wristband attached to a single silver key. Vince grabbed the key and stuffed it into his pocket, closing the drawer with his leg.

His eyes stared aimlessly at the ground as he pulled open the heavy front door of his residence. His lead Secret Service officer stood on the front walkway in a crisp suit.

"Sir, you heading out?"

Vince wagged his head. "Need to clear my head. You guys can hang here. I'm just walking around the observatory."

The officer offered a nod.

The heels of Vincent's shoes made muffled clacks on the dark, quiet asphalt surface as he rounded a turn to the right. The long white granite walls of the building lead up to a green copper roof. The building sat ominously illuminated at night from lights situated at ground-level. He enjoyed the observatory's simple isolation from the predatory feel of the surrounding city.

Vincent passed the main building and neared a stout, white, marble building that resembled a house with the same green copper roof and granite walls. Atop the building, however, sat a large, white sphere—the main covering of the MX7 telescope. He walked the sidewalk until he reached the white granite steps leading into the building. Vincent dug slowly into his pocket and found the stretchy, green keychain, and inserted the key into the door's lock.

It was dead quiet inside. Vincent flipped the lights on and took in a full breath. The room had been here for over a hundred years. The fourteen-foot-long telescope before him was one of the highlights of his tour of the grounds when he took office. A Naval officer had shown him how to work the entire building.

Vincent ambled over to a single chair positioned at the eyepiece of the massive telescope under the domed roof. He clicked a rectangular button on the floor with the toe of his shoe. Small motors buzzed to life and the slit in the dome appeared above him, allowing the telescope to see the night sky.

Vincent lowered himself into the wooden chair and leaned into the telescope's eyepiece. His eyes adjusted, and a bright star came into view. He reached up and rolled the large brass dial backward to zoom out further.

Rigel, Orion's brightest star. How fitting. The Archer.

Vincent thought about the Greek myth of Orion, the hunter who claimed to be the greatest, and was blinded for raping the granddaughter of the god Dionysus.

Vincent stared into the constellation, wishing he were no longer on earth. He leaned back into the wooden chair, reached into the pocket of his slacks, and withdrew his antique, black revolver.

CHAPTER 25

Belgrade, Serbia

Fixated on her iPad, Kelly poured through images of the Torlak Institute while Pierce updated Mariel.

She never imaged she'd be dealing with so much death at HIG. Her training taught her to manage it, but she had somehow believed it wouldn't be this prevalent in her work. The doctor who was killed in the street reminded her of her grandfather, and his eyes were kind, even as they laid his body into the grass.

HIG had sent her updated images and blueprints of the virology center. Kelly hoped the scientist who'd won the Nobel Prize wasn't involved in all this. Though after hearing her own vice president admit to what she assumed was sex with underage girls, she had to revisit her faith in government.

If this man had dirt on the vice president, she thought, then he's probably got his hands on a lot more people.

She zoomed in on an image of the virology research building where Doctor Nils had been worked. A rear door seemed to be the best entry point. The sun would rise up in a couple of hours. Emir brought the SUV to a stop on a dark road with tall trees and bushes on either side of them. Pierce ended the call with Mariel.

“Are we here?” Kelly asked.

Emir motioned out the passenger side of the windshield. “There is the institute, just a hundred meters this way on the right.”

“Pierce? Ready?” Kelly loaded her iPad into her slim briefcase and slid her Glock into its holster in the small of her back.

“Let's get in and out.” Pierce wrapped his earpiece behind his ear and tucked it in. Kelly did the same.

“I'll wait here. Want me to stay on the phone again?”

“Yes, I'll call you now.” Pierce dialed the phone and Emir placed it on speaker in his cup holder.

Pierce and Kelly walked down the asphalt road and reached a four-story building on their right.

“That's it,” Kelly announced. “Mariel, there's almost no security here. It's a little concerning. I wish we had a drone.”

"Copy. You guys do what you need to. Keep in mind there are five images we have of the building where a golf cart is visible in different locations. Might be security. There are two security guys at the main entrance on Vojvode stepe. One of them may be roving the grounds."

"Copy. There's a small fence here that couldn't even keep a dog out. We're going in through the back." Pierce's calm voice in her earpiece reassured Kelly as they leapt over the waist-high fence.

"Kelly, take point." Pierce pointed to a tiny white shack only ten yards away.

Kelly ducked down and kept low as she sprinted the short distance to the shack and took position. "Clear. Move."

Pierce came up beside her. "On you. Go ahead."

Kelly raced to the building's rear door only thirty yards away and flattened her back against the bricks in a narrow shadow the overhang created above the door. "Clear. Move." To her right, Kelly scanned the entrance beside her. Just beside the door, she noticed a keycard reader. She cursed under her breath. "Dammit. Mariel, we have a keycard access here. I thought the door would just be locked with a key lock."

Pierce made his way to Kelly and grabbed the taser out of his sling bag. He pressed the taser onto the maroon, metal keycard device and clicked the button. A crackle of blue light flashed, and a short beep emitted from the keypad. The small light on the keypad changed from red to green.

"No frickin' way. Mariel, never mind. We're in."

"Copy."

Without a sound, Pierce and Kelly crept to their left up four flights of stairs to the top floor. Nils' laboratory was located on the fourth floor at the end of the building. Kelly clicked on her small red flashlight to illuminate the dark hallway. The building was silent. The smell of iodine and rubbing alcohol hung in the cold air.

Kelly led the way past several doors on both sides, each of them equipped with a large rolling combination lock. They came to the final door on the right, dark grey and labeled with 'Nils Camus MD.' A yellow sticker below the label showed the international biohazard symbol. Kelly thought about the microscopic horrors that lay beyond the door. "How are we going to get into the lab? Mariel, we don't have any intel on these door combinations, do we?"

Kelly's earpiece beeped. "Sorry guys. No luck on that. What type of lock is it?"

"Looks like one of those X09 locks the military and CIA use," Pierce said.

"Okay. It's digital?"

"Yeah."

"Copy that. Let me look and I'll get back to you. Gimme about three—"

A loud, thundering crack jolted Kelly. Pierce had smashed his foot into the area just beside the doorknob, flinging the lab door open. Splinters of the wooden doorway littered the floor. "We're in, Mariel. No biggie."

Pierce glanced at Kelly. "The technology is newer than the building is."

He walked ahead of Kelly into the dark laboratory. Computers and machines rested on several tables aside glass testing equipment of all shapes and sizes. It reminded Kelly of the microbiology lab from college, where she'd decided to change her major from pre-med to psychology. Small fans in the equipment hummed in every corner of the room.

"What are we looking for, Mariel?" Pierce whispered as he leafed through a notebook on a desk, his dim, red flashlight glinting off the stainless-steel table.

Mariel replied in an instant. "Kelly, answer your phone."

Kelly's phone vibrated against her thigh. She answered the video call from HIG, turned the brightness on her screen down, and saw the face of Jason Mittenberg, the microbiology expert. "Hi, Kelly. Show me the lab, please," Jason muttered.

Kelly flipped the camera to face the lab. Her screen illuminated most of the room. She panned her phone around the dark room and Jason leaned into the camera, squinting through his reading glasses.

"Stop! Go over to that refrigerator." Kelly raised her head and wove through the steel tables to a glass-door refrigerator filled with samples, specimens, and assorted racks of labeled tubes.

Pierce handed her a set of purple disposable gloves from a nearby box with a shrug. "Never know." He took the phone from Kelly and pointed it at the fridge while she donned the gloves.

"Perfect. Now look for anything you can find that's sitting in a shallow Petri dish."

Kelly scanned the interior of the refrigerator through the glass door. "There's nothing like that in here."

Jason's voice quickened. "Okay, what about, like, a rack of little tubes with pointy bottoms. Do you see any of those?"

"Yeah. There's a little rack of those in here." Kelly shined her Gerber Recon flashlight through the glass door of the fridge, illuminating the small area in red light.

"Alright, now *very* carefully slide those out. Can you see labels on any of the tubes, or are any of the tubes a different color than the others?"

Kelly pulled open the door of the refrigerator. The interior light came on and flooded the room. She grabbed the little rack of tubes and slapped the door shut to kill the light. She rotated the head of her flashlight from red to white. A dim beam of light illuminated the rectangular rack filled with little plastic tubes. Every tube was filled with blue liquid except one.

“Jason, one of them looks brownish. All the others are like a clear blue liquid.”

Pierce held the phone’s camera up to the rack while Kelly illuminated it with her flashlight.

“Good. That’s what we need. Is there a label or number on the tube with the brown stuff in it?

Kelly leaned closer. “Yeah. The brown one says thirty-seven on it. Is that, like, a chemical code?”

“No. It’s just an identifier. Now, do you see any machines in there that look like a copy machine or fax machine?” Jason asked.

Kelly scanned the tables and found something that looked like a copy machine printer she used in the library at Georgetown. On the front, the large letters ‘REVSCI’ were printed on a label. “Is this it?”

Pierce swung the phone over to the machine and walked over to it.

“Yes! Great job. Now power it on. Just touch the screen.”

The screen came to life with a blue hue that illuminated their faces in the dark.

“It says ‘warm up.’”

“You can exit out of that. Just press the ‘X’ button. It will take you to the main page. Then you should see a menu. Look for something that says either 'history' or 'log.' Once you find that, lemme know what you see."

Pierce tapped on the machine while Kelly yanked the gloves off and pumped sanitizer into her hands from a nearby bottle near a sink.

"Okay, Jason. I'm in the history menu. What do I do?"

"Right. Just hold your phone at the screen where I can see it. I'll take screenshots. Keep hitting the 'Previous' button until you reach the end."

Pierce cycled through a series of what looked like jumbled numbers and letters with dates and times stamped at the bottom. A few dozen results later, Pierce reached the end of a list. Kelly aimed the phone at the screen, trying to keep it steady.

"Perfect," Jason chirped. "I think I've got what I need here. I can run all the codes through our database. You guys are good." He ended the video call with Jason, and Mariel's voice came through Kelly's earpiece.

"Thanks, guys. Get out of there."

As Kelly turned, a large figure stormed into the room holding a blinding flashlight. With an AK47 leveled at Pierce, the man began shouting in Serbian neither of them could understand.

CHAPTER 26

Belgrade, Serbia

The Russian Sukhoi Superjet 100 pounded onto the runway at Nikola Tesla Airport. Admiral Dimitri Kostyukov braved the flight, sitting next to an overweight man whose midsection encroached halfway into his seat. He had chosen to wear a simple button-down white shirt and dark blue blazer, opting for jeans instead of slacks.

He retrieved his leather carry-on bag from the overhead and ambled off the plane, silently cursing the undisciplined, slow Russians he had come to loathe over the years. His country was looking more like America every day.

In the terminal, four FSB officers stood casually dressed in suits for the admiral's arrival. They introduced themselves and one of the men reached for the admiral's bag. He refused the offer politely and walked out of the airport with the men to a waiting van. The admiral climbed into the front passenger seat and dismissed the pleasantries.

"What's going on here? Any word?"

The lead FSB officer in the rear seat scooted forward. "Admiral Kostyukov, we've received updates from many of our sources. I'm sure you're aware of the toxoplasma found in the submarines. As far as we can tell, there's no way for that to cause what happened in America. The two Serbian men lived here most of their lives. They didn't know each other until a month before they departed for Severodvinsk to work in the shipyard."

Dimitri turned toward the officer. "You've been able to trace them? What about their involvement with the submarines?"

"Yes, sir. They were being paid through a shell company based in Estonia called GreenTrend—they claim to specialize in solar technology. But the company is owned by a private trust. We called Moscow and they were able to uncover several names. They discovered the company is owned by another group called Grow Faction. It's based in New York. As far as we can tell, these Serbian men were paid to come to Severodvinsk and pollute the water supply and somehow make the submarines stay in port."

The admiral withdrew a Ziganov cigarette and lit it. "These people are staging a war. Our submarine fleet is mandated to stay in port for twenty-six more days for radiation testing because of the false results. We're powerless. If the Americans know this, they can cripple our fleet. We're sending our ships to their death, but we must show that we cannot be fucked with."

The young FSB officer cleared his throat and leaned a little further forward. "Admiral? The two Serbians from the shipyard—we found their apartments. They were littered with diagrams of the submarines, but we found something else. They had drawings of our *ships* in there too."

"Which ships?" Kostyukov demanded.

"Sir, we found water filtration diagrams from frigates, destroyer variants, and our carriers. Your Navy men provided us with more data on the Serbians as well. We know for sure they were on the Naval Base Severomorsk, and that they were on more than one ship. We have them on record going aboard the Destroyer Ushakov."

The van rolled into the fancy hotel entrance of the Belgrade downtown Hilton. Two valets opened the doors and allowed the men to exit with their bags.

An uneasy sensation crept into the admiral's mind. The Americans had to be involved somehow. He stared ahead at nothing as the group entered the hotel.

"Sir, we have a suite set up for you here. I am having the local police director come and speak with you."

He checked into his room, and two FSB officers entered with him, their guns drawn in what he assumed was more for show than security. He grabbed one of the men by the arm. “I’ve got to make decisions about our fleet in the next few hours. I need to get answers. Call back and have them run more tests on the water. Test everything. And find those men’s families. I don’t care if we need to drag them from their homes. The Americans are behind this. I know it.”

CHAPTER 27

Norfolk, Virginia

Jennifer Goram strode up the brick walkway to the Atlantic Fleet Headquarters building on Mitscher Avenue. Even at her age, she was still able to use her looks to her advantage. For that, she was grateful. Her blonde ponytail bounced as she strode to the tall glass door.

Just inside the building, a young sailor stood behind a security desk. Jennifer walked across a huge circular rug bearing the seal of the US Navy. Photos of ships and submarines dotted the walls behind the sailor, all centered around a carved wooden emblem on the wall that read 'Commander Naval Surface Force Atlantic Fleet.'

The young sailor greeted her, his eyebrows darting up.

Need for approval.

Jennifer approached the security desk with a raised hand.

Jennifer looked at the desk. A plastic nutrition shake mixer sat atop a paper towel, half-filled with red liquid. The sailor looked to be fit.

Works out—a lot. Need to feel powerful. Grew up with social anxiety. Responds well to authority when he's got permission.

"Do you remember the building number of the building two buildings to the left of that way?" Jennifer extended a hand, pointing in a random direction. "The little elementary school this way? Not a big deal. Thanks so much for all you **do. Incredible work . . . for me**, it's amazing. You guys are bad asses—Nelson! That's your name. So sorry." Jennifer leaned forward. The sailor glanced down at her cleavage. "I **get so turned around** on the base, but I asked for directions and they reassured me **everything is totally fine**. Once you get used to the base, it's a lot easier to **trust . . . me**, I even got lost in college when they **let me in** my freshman year."

The sailor blinked and tilted his head. Jennifer continued, "I'm with State Department, and was just here to visit with the Fleet Commander, Larry Trimble Thomas. It's hard to **admit . . . me**, I had no idea the base was so big. Even the security at the front gate. I'm glad they **let me right in**. Can you remind me which hallway I need to use?"

The bewildered sailor motioned to a hallway behind him. Jennifer placed a hand on his arm and thanked him. She strode around the security desk to the hallway on her left. Before she reached the entrance, the sailor shouted, “Hey! Ma’am?”

Shit.

Jennifer turned around to see the sailor standing with his hands on his hips. “I can’t let you back there without a visitor badge.” He picked up a green visitor badge from a box on the desk and walked it to Jennifer. “Sorry, must have forgot my head this morning.”

“Thanks Mister Nelson,” Jennifer said.

Jennifer took the badge and spun back to the hallway. She passed several offices and doors in the sterile, white hallway. More photos of Navy SEALs, divers, and sailors lined the halls. At the end of the long hallway, she found what she was looking for. Amidst the stark white tiles in the hall, a lone office sat at the end. A plush, red carpet lined on either side by decorative models of missiles.

Jennifer marched down the hallway, across the red carpet, and into a navy blue-trimmed door. A large brass plaque on the door read, Commander, U.S. Fleet Forces Command, Admiral Larry Trimble. The leader of the Navy. As a four-star admiral, the man commanded the entire fleet of the United States.

Jennifer stepped into the front office, where an older woman sat behind a fancy wooden desk. The bright blue carpet led to pristine white walls covered with framed awards and photos of navy ships. The woman stood. Jennifer raised a hand to prevent her from speaking and continued forward through the door leading to the admiral's office.

Admiral Larry Trimble sat behind his desk in a green camouflage uniform, speaking to a younger officer seated across his desk. Both men's attention snapped to Jennifer as she stepped into the room. She adopted a bold and erect posture. She sharpened her focus on the officer seated across from the admiral.

"Get out," Jennifer barked.

Without blinking, she stared the man in the eyes and pointed toward the door. Regardless of rank, Jennifer was surprised how people reacted to authoritative confidence. In the military, when someone didn't know who you were or what your rank was, they just defaulted to an obedient frame of mind.

The young man snatched a stack of papers as he shot out of his seat. He looked once at the admiral for confirmation, who was equally awestruck, and dashed to the door. Jennifer's eyes shifted directly to the Trimble's.

"Shut the door!" she barked over her shoulder as the man left the office.

The admiral hadn't said a word. The door clicked shut. Larry Trimble slowly set a pen down on his desk. "Just who the hell do you think—"

Jennifer held a finger up that stopped him short. "I'm here to save your life."

CHAPTER 28

Belgrade, Serbia

The angry Serbian holding the rifle at Pierce's face continued shouting frantically. Pierce slid the World Health Organization ID card from his pocket and held his hands in the air.

The guard stepped to the side and flipped on the light. Pierce approached, holding out his ID card, the other hand above his head.

"We're here to help!" Pierce took two more steps toward the man. He shook his rifle in warning as Pierce got to within three feet of him.

"*Ne prilazi! Odlazi! Oboje na kolenima!*" the guard continued to scream in Serbian. Pierce regretted not having a translator ready on the phone. The guard reached for his radio with the wrong hand - the one he shoots with.

Pierce shook his ID card, holding his arm stretched out to his right. The guard's attention shifted to the card. Pierce lunged forward into the guard. He grabbed the barrel of the man's rifle and jerked it violently upward toward the ceiling, then seized the butt of the weapon. He cracked the entire weapon into the man's forehead. The room fell silent again. The man laid motionless on the floor, blood oozing out of a deep gash in his forehead.

Kelly flicked the lights back off. "Is he dead?"

"Nah. He'll need stitches though. Universal healthcare benefits."

"We should call an ambulance for him. He's an innocent." Kelly stared at the bleeding man.

"You're kidding," Pierce insisted.

"No. We can't leave him here bleeding in the middle of a virology lab. Think about what he could get contaminated with in here!"

"Jesus. I'll put him out in the hall." Pierce grabbed the cuff of the man's right pant leg and towed him forward into the hallway. "Is that better?"

"Yes, dickhead." Kelly smiled and attempted to shut the crumpled door behind her.

Their earpieces simultaneously beeped. "Alright, guys. Jason found it. There's a spectrum code in the machine you just photographed. It is the third one you sent us a screen grab of. The logs for it go back five months. It's USP 5352181. Jason says this is a hybrid parasite with bad stuff in there. If you're still inside, get out."

Kelly's eyes widened at Pierce. "Let's go."

Mariel continued in their ears as they quietly descended the staircase in darkness. "The compound makes you thirsty, like crazy thirsty. Then it hijacks your brain to jump into the water and essentially drown yourself. That's what Jason has put together so far, anyway. Just as a precaution, Jason has advised you take a homemade antidote. If you're having symptoms like sudden mood changes and severe thirst, you need to get off the mission."

"Homemade antidote? *That* sounds fishy," Pierce whispered into his mic.

"Yeah. You need to eat a few matches." Mariel sounded as incredulous as Pierce.

Kelly rounded the final turn on the stairs and clicked her radio. "Wait. Like eating a match, like the things that start fires?"

"Yes, apparently so."

"Won't that kill you?"

"Kelly, you'd be surprised to know that when I was running an operation in Bogota, we would eat the heads of matches about every week or two to keep the mosquitoes off of us. It actually works." Pierce crept in the dark behind Kelly as she pushed open the back door they had entered through earlier.

Mariel continued, "So the sulfur and other stuff that's in the match will make your blood inhospitable for at least two of the parasites in the compound. Just eat a couple. Just the heads. You obviously aren't going to need the whole matchstick."

Pierce and Kelly ran through the grassy lawn to the low fence and hopped over. The sun illuminated the clouds as it rose.

Emir pulled the SUV alongside and they climbed in. "Sunrise should be in about forty-five minutes," Emir announced. He spun the vehicle around and sped off.

Mariel's voice came over the radio once more. "The Russian fleet is only a few hours from the shores here, guys. Do you know of Admiral Dimitri Kostyukov?"

"Yeah. The one who hates America and called for an all-out war?" Pierce muttered.

"Yeah. That one. We've just got word through CIA he's in town with you both. I'm willing to bet he's after the same evidence you are. He didn't announce the travel plans because he's probably trying to save face. Russia also hasn't announced the sailors testing positive for radiation sickness. He's probably gunning for the same person we are."

"Great. Now we've got to look out for this guy too?" Kelly asked.

"Well, not just him. He's got a Secret Service team with him. FSB. Probably all former KGB officers. Badasses. But you won't have to look out for him. You need to find his hotel room and talk to him."

Pierce buried his face in his hand. "Okay. Why?"

Kelly twisted to face Pierce; her eyebrows scrunched in confusion.

"The Americans can't reach the Russians. The Russian president hung up on our own president two hours ago. We *have* to de-escalate this. You need to join the Russians—we're both seeking the same goal, and the Russians have more resources in the area than we ever will."

"Copy all. We will get this done. Emir, let's head downtown."

"Thanks guys. The Russian admiral is at the Hilton hotel."

Mariel went silent for a moment. "Pierce? You guys will have to split up. Kelly can capture Ethan Peterson. He speaks English. She'll be able to use Tradecraft on him. I need you to find the Russian admiral and convince them to de-escalate the infantile politics. If this chemical stuff is on the Russian ships, we need to explain this wasn't us, and let them know they're in serious danger."

Kelly nodded, flicking hair from her face. "I'm good with that. I'll take Ethan down."

"Okay, Kelly. The house is just across the Street from the American Embassy. Large, white mansion. His bodyguards are Americans too as far as I know—they speak English."

Pierce shook his head. “I don’t know if this is the best way to do this, Mariel. If we stay together—”

“If you stay together, you’ll have *twice* the work. *Double* the amount of time. The Russian fleet is already within striking distance from the shore. The admiral is hell-bent on proving himself. Kelly will be fine.”

Kelly straightened. “I’m right here. And yes, I’ll be fine.” She put a hand on Pierce’s leg. “I’ll head there now, Mariel.”

The turn signal seemed to send Pierce’s attention forward, out the windshield. Emir had heard the new information and was already changing course toward the Embassy area of town. Emir passed a City Records building and turned left around a roundabout.

“We’re about three minutes from there,” Emir announced.

Kelly leaned back in the seat, reached underneath her tight shirt, and unhooked her bra. “Here we go.”

CHAPTER 29

Norfolk, Virginia

Admiral Trimble hadn't been spoken to in this tone in decades. He had commanded a Guided Missile Destroyer, a Cruiser, and the entire Atlantic Fleet. This woman was either crazy or extremely powerful.

In three confident strides, the woman sliced through his office and dropped into the wooden chair in front of his desk. She crossed her legs, barely covered by her slitted business skirt, her breasts straining against the slim, white collared shirt she wore.

She's not crazy, that's for sure.

"Admiral, I need your undivided attention." The woman's voice was a hornet's nest.

Larry took in a breath and leaned onto his desk. "Well, you've just kicked out the Deputy Chief of

Naval Operations. And he shut the door for you. So, you've got my attention."

The woman smiled; her gentle gaze transmitted a motherly warmth as she spoke. "The Russian fleet will be on our shores in less than seven hours. I took an oath to keep this from happening, and I'm going to do just that."

"Okay, Miss . . ."

"My name is Jennifer. Jennifer Goram. I work for an agency that doesn't just protect *this* country; we protect them all. We have people in Russia now. The stuff you found in the water wasn't just Toxoplasma gondii. It was spliced with another parasite called a hairworm. Another compound was added that deregulates cellular osmolality."

"Osmolality?"

"Basically, how your cells tell you when they need water or not. It's what made the Russian crew jump off the submarine."

Trimble adjusted in his chair. "Ma'am. I don't know who you are, but we've got advanced laboratories that—"

"That don't test for this specific parasite whatsoever."

Trimble wrote a quick note on a pad and nodded. "Miss Jennifer, what you saw in Norfolk was indicative of three things. First, the Russians were operating well within our territorial waters. Second, this is the first time Russian nuclear missiles have touched American soil. This is an intelligence goldmine. Third, this is a deliberate setup by the Russians to incite a war. We are going to have to respond to this action. We can't have a Russian fleet out here with no response. Our ships are getting underway to respond as we speak."

Jennifer scooted forward in her chair. "If you respond to this, there's a ninety-five percent chance we'll wind up in a nuclear war."

Trimble shook his head. "Do you realize the Russians are responding to this incident by arming *Iran*? They are moving missiles to Iran and North Korea as we speak. They won't have to engage with us—they're going to let these other countries run by absolute dipshits do all the work."

"Admiral, let me be crystal clear here." She tilted forward and captured Larry's gaze. "There's something underneath everything you're not considering, and the foundation of what happened yesterday continues to run forward when it's back to—you can **become completely open to this** is something you can **let go . . . now, with me**, I can see how easy it is to imagine **everything unraveling** . . . is what **you feel . . . completely fine** with absolute **open . . . you're mine** is going to play tricks on you."

Trimble felt his face softening. The woman continued the barrage. "When I learned about this, I was shocked as well. It becomes one of those things that **haunts you** . . ." Jennifer subtly pointed to herself. ". . . and only until you **completely let go. Now, with me**, it's something that can really **open**

your mind...To me, I really was able to **feel every single word penetrate** when I read the report as well. So many of the officers who work for you get into trouble when they don't **listen to this inner voice** . . ." Jennifer gestured to her mouth. ". . . that guides them. We all have one. It's like when you **realize that *this* voice is here to guide you**, and we get into huge trouble when we don't **listen to it**. When you **hear this voice, you don't hesitate, you act**. That's why you've been so successful. You can **act on this without thought or hesitation**. You're hearing **this voice** even now."

Jennifer stood and stepped around the desk. Trimble looked up at her through a fog. She stuck out her hand. "I'm so sorry, I forgot to introduce myself. I'm Jennifer." As Trimble instinctively stuck out his hand, she gently clutched his wrist and lifted his hand toward the ceiling. The mysterious woman commanded, "Look at your hand." She moved his hand slowly toward his face.

For some reason, he did as she asked. She continued, "Let it all go. Eyes closed."

An unusual sensation crept through him. His body drifted downward into some sort of abyss. Floating somehow. It was the most peaceful thing he'd felt in years.

Peace.

"And that's an overview of our products and services!" The woman's voice crashed through his mind and brought him back into the office. She was seated across from him now.

"Oh—Okay. Thank you, Miss . . . ."

"Wallace." She hopped out of her chair like a nimble teenager and walked to the door.

"Thanks for your time, Admiral! Sorry to barge in." She turned with a bright smile and waved as she left the office.

Trimble checked his watch. Thirty-six minutes had passed.

CHAPTER 30

Belgrade, Serbia

Kelly climbed out of the back seat onto the road a block away from The Archer's mansion. Pierce held her gaze as though they were parting ways indefinitely, like he was memorizing the way she looked.

"I'll be fine." She adjusted her shirt and threw the strap of her small, leather purse over her shoulder. The morning sun filtered through the clouds above, painting the street in pallid light.

"I have no doubt. Call if you need anything."

"If anyone there speaks English at all, there won't even be an issue." Kelly flashed him a grin and winked as she shut the door.

She shut the door and the SUV sped off. Pierce would worry, she knew. She was walking into a viper pit of sexual predators with no mission, planning, or preparation. She glanced down. Her breasts were visible through her white shirt. If the rain came back, it would certainly make things more interesting.

Cars buzzed past as she stepped over puddles on the sidewalk. To Kelly's right, a quaint neighborhood bar by the name of *Lounge Bar Baza* was opening for business as employees wiped rain off outdoor tables. She strode to the corner and passed a tiny convenience store that was more of a shack than a building. Two men holding paper cups of coffee raised their heads and stared as she passed.

Kelly turned right on Šolina. Fifty yards ahead, she came upon a white stone wall that surrounded the sprawling compound occupied by the man who terrified the vice president. A white pole sprouted from beyond the wall, topped with a security camera. Kelly continued forward to a black iron gate. A muscular security guard stood before the gate, a black wire poking from his collar and curling into his ear.

His attention shifted to her, down to her breasts, and back to her face. The man eyed Kelly as she strode toward him. Kelly did her best to exude a confident, bouncy stride, keeping with the clientele who frequented this house. As she neared, he turned to face her fully and addressed her in Serbian.

"Dobro jutro. Ko si ti?"

He's not American.

Kelly smiled and forced a cheery tone to broadcast naivete. "So sorry. I don't speak the language here. I wish I did."

"Ah. You're American. Sorry. What can I do for you?" the man replied in perfect, American English.

Kelly raised her eyebrows. Her dimples on full display. "Well, you could open the gate."

"Of course. You're here for massage, or . . . ?"

"You got it. Assuming I'm still booked for now?" Kelly glanced at her Raymond Weil Freelancer watch, making sure the man saw it. He did.

"Let me check and make sure. One moment."

Shit.

The man reached for his radio mic. Kelly scanned him. The heel of his right shoe was worn at an angle.

Right knee problems.

A gold ring embedded with diamonds encircled his pinky.

Needs to feel significant. Probably has concealed envy about his boss' money.

A spider web tattoo jutted upward from the man's collar.

Thrives on feeling powerful. Likely childhood trauma or bullying.

Kelly took what little of the man's behavioral profile she had and leaned forward and touched his bicep. "Holy shit. You're strong!" As reluctant as the man was, Kelly knew she just flooded his brain with pleasure chemicals. She took a small step forward. “What’s your name again?”

“Ian.”

“Ah. Ian. Love it.” Kelly gestured to herself as she said the words. “Look, it’s easy to completely separate the part listening closely, and not actually doing than the part that isn’t not completely focused. And it’s easy to **just relax** into knowing that **you have so little control**. It’s such a good feeling to just **lose yourself** into what **captures all of your focus** . . .” Kelly pointed subtly to herself. “. . . when nothing can become what you aren’t noticing. And my friend said, **just relax. Now**, when I try to think about too many things at once, I **get absolutely distracted** so much that it’s one of those moments when you **let go completely**.” Kelly tugged Ian’s wrist downward and spoke reassuringly into his ear. “It’s completely fine. Perfect.” His head slumped forward a little. She continued. “It’s easy to notice now that **everything is totally fine**. You’re **absolutely fine** and I was just going inside this way through this gate. And how does it open again, Ian?

The man dug into his pocket and squeezed something that clicked. An electric motor whirred, and the heavy iron gate lurched into action.

“Thanks, Ian. You were just letting them know I was coming in? Is that right?” She gestured to his radio. Ian nodded and cupped his hand over his mic.

"One through the gate. It's a Miami."

Kelly assumed 'Miami' was some code for massage or what type of girl was coming into the house. She hoped it didn't mean middle-aged woman.

She scanned the house. The two-story mansion's white concrete walls gave way to arched windows and elaborate second-floor balconies. Stoic columns rose in formation around a covered entryway. Kelly strutted across the brick driveway and up several steps to the front door. An electronic buzz sounded. The door clicked open. She reached down with her left hand, and once again with her right, creating a fresh muscle memory to the location of the SOCP dagger tucked into the front of her skirt.

Her stomach sank. She suddenly realized she had no idea who laid in wait on the other side. She'd seen the man she was about to capture on television so many times. The billionaire investor who spun off multi-level marketing companies like a factory. His reach, however, was outside the awareness of the public.

He's more powerful than any president.

Kelly cleared her throat and pushed through the heavy door. The cool air in the house spilled out onto her feet. The entryway was castle-like. Kelly imagined the people who had been through it. The women who were hauled in and out of here. Her spine tingled at the thought.

Two circular, stone staircases led up to the second floor before her. In the center of the large foyer, a heavy marble table sat centered on an ornate Persian rug with an oversized vase of flowers at its center. The tan marble floors joined taupe walls dotted with paintings of nude women in suggestive poses. The house was silent.

On the second floor, Ethan emerged from a bedroom wearing a white bathrobe. "Just who the fuck are you?"

His artificially tanned skin showed from beneath the robe. He titled his head, examining her. The man's face was long and aged. White tendrils grew from his eyebrows.

Kelly eyed the man. Vulgar grey hairs sprouted across his chest, almost enveloping a gold chain necklace. "They booked me for a massage. I know I'm a little early. Sorry."

She sized the man up. She'd need to play this from a little-girl angle until she could wrap this piece of shit up.

"Did Tiffany book you to come out?"

Kelly weighed her options. Having no intelligence on the man, she'd have to tiptoe through the next few minutes. She had to get him downstairs, or she had to get upstairs.

"Yes. It was Tiffany, far as I know."

"Okay. Great." Ethan sauntered down the stairs. His unflinching eyes on her chest felt like prickly, nauseating fingers. He rounded the base of the stairs and stopped, standing across the massive foyer from Kelly with his hand resting on the granite bannister.

"You're a sweet little piece of action. You know that?" He offered a one-sided smile of bleached teeth, his eyes narrowed. Ethan withdrew a phone from the pocket of his robe and began typing on the screen with both thumbs.

Kelly forced a giggle and looked away. "Thanks, sir."

"Who told you I like to be called sir? Tiffany?" he said, continuing to type on his phone. A smirk grew on his face.

"Yeah. Is that okay?" Kelly arched her eyebrows, feigning innocence.

"Of course! That's great. I only have one issue, aside from you marching your perky little ass in here before our appointment."

"Issue?" Kelly forced a look of calm as her heart pounded so hard it felt like her pulse was visible from across the room.

"Yep. I don't have anyone named Tiffany. And I prefer 'savior,' not 'sir.'" His eyes darted over Kelly's shoulder and he nodded.

Before she could turn, a stabbing pain tore through the side of her neck and jolted her head back. She spun around to see an older woman holding a plastic syringe. Her head tilted in disapproval.

Hot lead filled Kelly's insides. She wobbled to the left, and the swelling weight of her body tugged her to the cold floor. Her knees crashed onto the tile, but they were far away. She drew in a deep, thick breath. Her face pressed onto the tile. The muscles in the side of her neck struggled to lift her head.

If this were poison, she'd only have a moment to use Tradecraft.

She screamed Phrase One.

At the base of the staircase, Ethan's fuzzy form stood with limp arms. Behind her, the older woman mumbled, her speech slurring, stuttering, until it became a soft, drunken warble that threatened to lull Kelly to sleep.

It worked.

They were limp, dangling. But there was something *else* she was supposed to say. Like a follow-up. To make it take full effect.

The cold marble floor felt wonderful on her cheek. Safe.

Then the woman's voice echoed in the foyer as she came out of it. "Wow. What the hell was that? What the *hell* did you do, little girl?"

Kelly knew she shouldn't, but somehow, she enjoyed the feeling of the smooth marble.

Ethan, still blurry, shook his head. He stumbled toward Kelly. "*What* did you do to me?"

His face grew angry as he neared Kelly. He looked to the older woman behind her. “Get the helicopter ready. This little bitch needs to disappear.”

As he knelt beside her, a wave of warmth wrapped around her body.

She didn’t know what he meant. She could rest. She faded into the floor, smiling.

CHAPTER 31

Belgrade, Serbia

This could be the dumbest thing I've ever done, and the last thing I do.

Pierce walked into the Hilton hotel lobby and approached the long, wooden check-in desk. Muted conversations bounced off the gray marble walls. A short man behind the desk in a black vest greeted him in English. He knew he couldn't ask for a room number, and it was likely the Russian admiral was staying under a false name, as Pierce had done hundreds of times.

"How many suites do you have here in the hotel?"

The check-in clerk typed away on his keyboard. "It looks like we have five open suites, sir."

"Thank you, but how many are there in total? My wife and I need something specific."

"Sir, we have six in total."

"Great. Thank you. We were hoping for a suite facing downtown." Pierce swept his hand toward the downtown area.

The clerk typed on the keyboard once more. "Yes, we have two that face downtown directly. One of them is open. It's on the fifth floor, sir."

"Thanks, we can't book the suite on the sixth floor, can we?"

"No, sir. I'm afraid that one is booked already."

"Thanks. I'll be back."

Pierce turned. The admiral would most likely use a suite. He'd have guys with him too. Pierce strode through the sunlit lobby to the row of slick, black elevator doors. He punched the elevator call button. The doors slid open. He stepped in and pressed the 'six' button with the back of his hand.

On the short elevator ride, Pierce rotated his black sling bag from his back to hang at his chest. He had no idea what to expect. He unzipped the compartment containing his Glock, and ran his finger along the side, confirming a round was chambered. He left the zipper open and opened another, producing a short titanium pry bar only five inches long. The small pry bar was a standard-issue tool for HIG. The thing had myriad uses and had saved his ass on many occasions.

Before the doors slid open, Pierce checked his phone. Nothing from Kelly. His jaw tightened.

The elevator dinged. The polished doors slid apart onto the sixth floor, opening to gray carpet.

Pierce exited and entered the hallway to the right. The admiral's suite was the last door on the right. He strode down the hallway, his heartrate increasing as he ran through scenarios of what might happen when confronting a Russian admiral who despised the United States.

He arrived at the door.

627

With no idea what he was walking into, and no plan whatsoever, Pierce inhaled sharply, and let out a long, steady breath. He reached up and knocked on the door.

Commotion ensued behind the door. Two deep voices communicated quietly in Russian. The handle clicked, and the door opened several inches. A muscular Russian man peered through the crack, careful not to reveal the room behind him.

"*Šta hoćeš?*"

Pierce raised his hands, keeping his right hand lower, closer to the weapon in his bag. "Sorry, I don't speak Russian."

The man examined him from top to bottom and replied in choppy, broken English. "It *wasn't* Russian. It was Serbian. Why would you think it was Russian?"

Pierce exhaled through a clenched jaw; he'd made a mistake. "Listen. I need to speak with the admiral."

The Russian tilted his head. "Who the hell are you? What admiral?"

"Admiral Dimitri Kostyukov."

He eyed Pierce with a narrow squint. "Are you American?"

"Yes."

"Government, CIA . . . ?"

"No."

"You carrying a weapon?"

"Yes. Glock G45. It's in this bag here." Pierce kept his palms in the air.

"Give me the bag. Keep your right hand up where it is."

Pierce kept his right hand up and clicked the magnetic lock on the strap with his left, releasing the bag from his body. He passed the bag to the man behind the door. The man took it without breaking eye-contact. Pierce assumed the man held a gun of his own behind the door with his other hand. The Russian yanked the sling bag through the opening and slammed the door shut.

Pierce's muscles tightened as he waited for the man in the room to rummage through his belongings. Luckily, the hallway remained empty. After a moment, the door swung open. The Russian stood casually inside the doorway holding a

Makarov pistol. Pierce put his hands back above his head.

"Turn around," the man barked, his expression still detached.

Pierce slowly turned his back on the man. The FSB officer patted him down, even checking his hair, his shirt collar, and inside his ears.

"Okay. Come in. You know this man doesn't like Americans, yes?"

"I've been told." Pierce followed the officer into the room. The admiral sat cross-legged in a turquoise chair, and two other FSB Officers sat across from him on a matching-color couch.

The admiral's short, grey hair and weathered skin betrayed his decades-old relationship with the sea. The amused smile on his face only worried Pierce more. The two FSB officers were equally unimpressed with his entrance.

The admiral uncrossed his legs and stood. "Please have a seat." He gestured to the vacant area on the couch between the two FSB officers. Pierce reluctantly wedged himself between them. They remained silent and motionless. The heavier one on his left was still in good shape, with a grey beard. The man on his right looked like an athlete, fit. All the FSB men wore black.

The admiral opened his hands. "I honestly cannot imagine the circumstances that would lead to you coming into this room. I'm very curious to know. This says you work for World Health

Organization. Is this true?" The admiral's English was impressive. Almost fluent.

Pierce shook his head. "No, Admiral. The ID is fake. My real name is Pierce Reston. I'm a member of an intelligence agency organization based in the US, but we don't work for the Americans. I came here to stop you from starting a war. America was *not* behind your submarine incident. I've been aboard the sub. One of your sailors is alive. The submarine wasn't completely empty."

The old man's eyes expanded. "The Americans have been doing this shit for decades, Mister Reston. There's nothing you can say that will change my mind. You're wasting your time here. More importantly, you're wasting *mine*."

Pierce swallowed hard. "Admiral. I'm willing to bet you're here looking for someone. The two Serbian men who died in Severodvinsk. They had financial backing from a shell company here."

Kostyukov had a good poker face, but HIG's training gave Pierce a superpower—no one could hide their feelings if you knew how to see them. The admiral's lips tightened only slightly.

Withheld opinions.

Pierce continued. "The shell company is owned by proxy—by an American. He's financed this shit for God knows what, but the government isn't involved. I'm also willing to bet you've found *Toxoplasma gondii* in the water supply of a few subs and ships."

Kostyukov's lips squeezed together again. The small muscle in the center of his chin tightened. "We have," he admitted.

Withheld opinions; shame.

"Good. Call them back and have them test it again if you'd like. It's not just *Toxoplasma gondii*, it's worse. It was spliced with another parasite called a hairworm. We believe the men installed devices on your ships that have a type of timing release that discharges the bioweapon at certain times. That explains why other ships haven't had it yet."

"They have."

Pierce eyed the admiral in silence. The men on either side of Pierce remained motionless.

The admiral's head fell as a breath escaped. "Two of my other submarines are missing."

"Jesus. We have the compound that can kill the parasite, but the ships need to be in port to do it. Admiral, if we continue, you may lose way more than a couple of submarines. You could lose a Navy if this stuff is widely distributed. The sailor we saved from the submarine in Norfolk is healthy. He testified that the men jumped to their deaths. He wasn't affected until later due to high sulfur levels in his blood."

"I'm not bringing an entire fleet into harbor like a dog with its tail between its legs." He turned to the officer on Pierce's left. "Call Moscow. Tell them to test for hairworm in the water of every ship."

"Are you CIA, Mister Reston?" The admiral's eyebrows narrowed as he waited on Pierce's response.

"No. I get paid a lot more than that. You may not have time to test all your ships. It would be more embarrassing to have all your sailors jumping overboard on the US coastline."

"You told me you know where this man is who orchestrated this?"

"Yeah. It's Ethan Peterson. He's here in town now. We have someone there taking him into custody as we speak. I'm happy to hand him over to you, but we'd like to know why this happened, and if there's more to the plan than we've realized as of yet."

"Ethan Peterson, the American businessman? You think *he's* behind this?"

"I can prove it, sir. But I need your help to de-escalate this incident. I've got someone at his home now, capturing him."

"It appears we may have similar interests."

"More than you know. My agency is the reason the truck with the chemical weapons bound for Moscow crashed into the Moscow Canal in March of 2013."

The old man's eyes searched Pierce's face. He let the moment become uncomfortable before he replied. "That's classified information. How do you know about this?"

"I *made* it crash, Admiral. We had to keep the weapons wet to prevent an aerosol dispersal."

"That information was never released. Tell me, where *exactly* did the truck crash?" The old man leaned forward, his gaze sharpening.

"I forced it off the road just southwest of a bus station on A104. It was in about seven feet of water. I rolled it on its side to make sure the weapons were completely submerged."

Kostyukov lowered his head and grunted at the floor. "If this is true, you saved thousands of Russian lives, Mister Reston," he said in a resigned tone.

"Thanks, Admiral. I'm not looking for accolades here. I'm trying to save even more lives. Russian lives."

"If what you are saying is correct about these hairy worms . . ." The admiral's voice trailed off.

"We can make your sailors safe," Pierce reassured him. "I'm heading to Ethan Peterson's house now. It's across the street from the US Embassy here."

"My men will join you, if you don't mind. I'm going to wait to hear back from my own scientists who will perform this testing on the water."

Pierce glanced at one of the FSB men standing beside the couch. The man's face had softened a little. He extended a hand to Pierce. "I'm Vlad. This is Yuri and Boris."

Pierce shook their hands. "I'm glad you all speak English. Thank you. I'd be happy to have you guys with me."

"All spies speak English, Pierce. And *every* country spies on America."

Pierce's phone dinged. Yuri, the man holding his sling bag, took a step forward and handed it over. Pierce withdrew his phone and tapped the screen. A message from Mariel.

Kelly is either missing, or out of contact.

CHAPTER 32

Belgrade Serbia

Kelly was being lifted. Carried. The roar of an engine permeated the air around her. Powerful wind whipped hair into her face from above. She rotated her head around, searching for the source of the engine noise.

"We're going to the yacht," Ethan yelled to a man opening the pilot's door of a gray helicopter.

It's a helicopter.

The man stared at Kelly. "She okay?"

"Yeah. She overdosed downstairs but she's fine. She's coming with us on the yacht to get over it."

Kelly felt muscular arms lower her face down into a long, tan leather seat. The older woman scooted into the seat beside her and brushed hair from her face. "You're a *cutie*! You know that?"

She turned her head. Through a cloudy haze, she saw a pilot climb into a seat. Ethan hopped into a seat facing Kelly, still wearing the white bathrobe. He nodded to the older woman through a pair of aviator sunglasses. "Maxie, did you grab the party kit?"

The woman, Maxie, dug into her purse and withdrew a little black Hermès zipper bag.

Ethan nodded and swirled a short glass filled with ice as he climbed in and sat opposite Kelly. "She may need a little push. Take her picture first while her eyes are open. We'll send it to the group. Someone may want to purchase."

Maxie tilted over Kelly, held her phone sideways, and snapped a few pictures. Kelly eyed the sparkling phone case. Glitter danced around in a liquid inside the fancy-looking case. It was fascinating. Maxie sat back in her seat and tapped on her phone again. "Honey, do you speak any other languages?"

Kelly managed a small nod. "Spanish and French." The detached words crept from her mouth.

Maxie pulled Kelly's feet into her lap and slipped off one of her shoes. A sharp pinch near her ankle snapped Kelly's attention to Maxie. The woman gripped a skinny syringe at an angle and plunged the contents into a vein in Kelly's foot.

The heavy weight climbed through her body again. Kelly plopped her head back on the seat.

The quick, upward force of the helicopter taking off exhilarated her.

Kelly lifted her leaden head and dragged her gaze up to Ethan, who sat with legs spread in his seat. His bathrobe parted between his legs. His head turned to Kelly. He eyed her for a moment through his sunglasses with a smirk.

"Do I need to buckle up for safety?" Kelly murmured. It was her own voice, but it sounded foreign, deeper.

The woman patted her on the butt. "You're fine. We're already almost there."

A moment later, the helicopter trembled downward. Landing. Maxie lowered Kelly's legs to the floor. "I'm going to hold onto your shoes, honey. You can walk barefoot."

The engine wound down with a whine. Ethan popped the door open and stepped out into the grey morning weather. Maxie threw Kelly's arm around her shoulder and lifted, half-dragging her out of the helicopter onto short grass. Kelly shifted her feet and struggled to stand.

The grass under her feet gave way to a long, paved pier along a wide river. A single building to her right with tables and chairs overlooking the waterway.

A man in a Chef's uniform climbed out of a nearby car and passed the trio. "Hi, Mister Peterson!" The chef exclaimed. "Would you like me to bring over food from the restaurant for the trip today?"

Ethan shook his head. "Hey, man. Good to see you. We loaded up the kitchen on the boat yesterday, but thanks for the offer."

The chef angled his head at Kelly. "My goodness. Is she alright?"

"Oh, yeah. She's had a few too many mimosas this morning. She's one of my interns."

The chef offered a puzzled look and departed toward his restaurant. Kelly's head slumped. She'd never felt so at peace. Dizzy, but peaceful. The grass under her feet turned to cold stone. She forced her head up again. Tied to the pier, a behemoth grey yacht dominated the landscape.

Maxie smelled like lavender and lime. The wind blew strands of her short black hair onto Kelly's cheek. "Almost there, honey. Keep your head up; it'll stop the spins."

They boarded the yacht and a crew member in a fitted, white uniform greeted Ethan and Maxie. "Good morning! Are we leaving port?"

Ethan stepped ahead and placed a hand on the crew members stark white shirt. He spoke quietly into his ear; the man nodded.

The men walked across a short, noisy aluminum walkway onto the polished wood deck of the yacht. Maxie placed a hand on Kelly's back, prodding her forward across the walkway and up to a large sliding-glass door at the rear of the boat.

Ethan slid the door open. Maxie ushered Kelly through the doorway into an opulent dining room area with dark red carpeting and tables set with crystal and flowers. They walked through the dining room into a living area dotted with silver sculptures of nude women, a few paintings, and a long, white leather couch.

"Can I lay down?"

Maxie nudged her toward the couch. "Sure, honey. Go right ahead."

Kelly let her body unfold on the couch. Her eyes were heavy. She permitted them to close for a moment. It felt good. The couch embraced her with a kindness she couldn't define.

Ethan's voice came from behind. "Strip her down and get photos. We need to find out who she is. If she's not government, I got an interested buyer in Dubai who wants to see her whole body."

CHAPTER 33

Belgrade, Serbia

"Are you okay, man?" The Russian FSB officer tilted his head at Pierce.

Pierce's chest filled with heat. His stomach tightened into oak. He raised his head to the Russian admiral now standing before him. "Do you mean what you say about these men assisting me?"

"I mean it insofar as what you've told me is the truth. As far as the Navy is concerned, I'm—"

"Good. I have an operative who was at Ethan's house. She's now missing, with Ethan. This is the man who's paid for your fleet to be poisoned. I'd like to find him."

Pierce knew Tradecraft would work on the admiral, but the other men in the room who didn't speak fluent English would immediately notice the man's sudden shift in behavior.

The admiral glanced around at the spies surrounding him. "Go bring me that fucking snake."

Everyone in the room stood. The FSB men took turns shaking Pierce's hand. The admiral said something to them in Russian as they left.

"*U nas yest' obshchiy vrag. Ne podvedi svoyu okhranu po lyuboy prichine.*"

Pierce didn't understand, and couldn't have cared less. He fought to push the thoughts of Kelly from his mind.

Before they exited, the admiral called out, "Pierce Reston. I thank you for your service to our country. However, I will not publicly allow Americans to offer assistance to the Russian fleet. I wish you all good luck. *Udachi tebe.* As we say in Russia, Mister Reston."

The admiral stood before the small hotel room desk with his hands clasped in front of his crotch.

Insecurity or vulnerability.

Outside the hotel, Vlad placed a hand on Pierce's shoulder and motioned across the valet area to a black Mercedes van. "This is our car."

The van was parked beside Emir's SUV. Emir was patiently sitting in the driver's seat and waved to Pierce.

"Is this your man?" Vlad asked. He flipped the collar of his black jacket up.

"Yeah. He's a driver we hired here locally. I'm just going to grab a bag from the car."

"If you have a driver, we can ride with you. Faster."

Pierce raised an eyebrow at the officers. "You guys have any gear?"

In unison, the three men chuckled. "We will be fine," Vlad said with a smile. He turned and barked at the two other officers. "*Poluchi nashi sumki!*"

Yuri and Boris trotted to their black van and withdrew three large duffel bags. Pierce angled his head to the driver's window of the Expedition. Emir's face lit up as he rolled the window down.

"You made some new friends!"

"They're Russian...FSB."

Emir's jaw dropped. He turned and looked at the men in black leather jackets and black pants carrying bags to the rear of his own vehicle with an entirely new expression. "My god. They are James Bond people."

Pierce didn't hear him. His thoughts went to Kelly—the man who called himself the Archer had made the worst mistake of his life. Pierce contemplated finding the man—making him eat his own arms off.

He settled into the second row with Vlad. Yuri sat next to Emir, who was already eyeing the men like celebrities. Boris climbed in the back by Vlad.

"Where are we going?" Emir glanced at Pierce in the rear-view mirror.

"Same place you dropped off Kelly—she's missing."

Emir gripped the wheel and the SUV launched forward into the streets. He wove skillfully through traffic, keeping his speed in check.

"Pierce. Sorry about before. Americans aren't seen the same way in this corner of the world," Vlad explained.

"It's fine. I would have done the same. I'm grateful you guys are here."

The vehicle sped around a corner. "Russia isn't as bad as you think. We do a lot of good work. Most of the time, our military is protecting other countries or helping with disaster relief around the world," Vlad said.

"I know it. You don't have to convince me. It's the American propaganda machine. Both of us have propaganda; Russia just has the balls to admit it. People in America criticize you guys for having 'state-owned' television, controlled by the government, but it's exactly what we have; we just pretend it isn't."

Vlad smiled. Yuri twisted in his seat to face them. "I worked the intelligence on the chemical weapons truck you crashed in the river. I can tell you, if that truck was not in water, the weapons would have been released. You did save a lot of people, Mister Reston."

"Stopping where I dropped her off?" Emir interrupted.

The Russian spies looked to Pierce, who was glared through the windshield. “No. Go right to the god-dammed door.”

Emir took another turn as Boris passed two Heckler & Koch MP5s to the others. The small submachine guns were equipped with fat, grey silencers.

“You need a gun?” Vlad said to Pierce.

“No. I’ll just talk to them. They are Americans.”

“Because they are *Americans,* they will not hurt you?” Vlad chuckled.

“I’ll see what happens. I have the Glock if I need it.”

Yuri shook his head. “I will watch this. Very funny.”

“Okay!” Emir interrupted. The vehicle lurched to a stop, a white granite mansion on their left. A large, muscular guard stood in a suit beside a black iron gate. He peered into the tinted windows of the SUV.

Yuri erupted from the passenger door and leveled his silenced weapon at the man’s head. Vlad and Pierce burst out of the rear doors. The guard’s hands instinctively jerked toward his firearm.

Vlad stopped him short with a quick ‘sssssst’ sound. The man’s hand shot into the air. The Russians concealed the weapons at their sides.

"Put your hands down! Someone's going to think we are robbing you, idiot," Vlad spat.

The guard's hand lowered. He clenched his jaw as Vlad spoke, eyeing him at an angle.

Pierce stepped forward and put his mouth by the man's ear and uttered Phrase Three, followed by several surgically crafted commands.

The guard's head fell and bounced on his broad chest. Two seconds later, he adjusted his posture, smiled, and opened the gate. "Right this way, gentlemen."

He led the way across the driveway as the Russians exchanged confused glances. Pierce tucked in behind the guard, matching his stride.

The guard typed a code into the keypad. Pierce memorized it. 12014.

The door swung open and the Russians raised their weapons as they flooded into the foyer. Their safety switches clicked off simultaneously.

"Where is Kelly?" Pierce shot at the guard.

"Th—the woman who was here for the massage?" The guard's brows raised. "They all left in the helicopter like forty-five minutes ago. They went northeast, probably to the boat."

"What boat?"

"Mister Peterson keeps a boat—a yacht—here. He takes it up the river on weekends for, like, parties and stuff."

"Up the Danube river?"

"Yeah."

"When you say 'up,' you mean north?"

The guard shrugged. "Oh. No. I don't know for sure."

"Where's the boat kept? What kind of helicopter?"

"It's on the pier right outside of Imperium Caffe. And I think it's an Airbus?"

Pierce scowled. "You let little girls in here a lot?"

"I mean, yes. They're young. I don't know how old."

Pierce took the opportunity to stab a few more questions. "What's the youngest?"

The guard's hands went up in surrender. "Well . . . maybe, like twelve?"

"You're going to do me a big favor. Go find the evidence in this house for all of that while I'm gone and then stand right here in this foyer until I come back. Videos, tapes, recordings, photos. All of it. I don't care if you have to eat or piss. You stand right here after you're done. Pile it all on the table and stand *right here* when you're done. Understand?"

"Of course. Yes. I will." The man nodded slowly. The onlooking Russians stared in awe as the man marched up the stairs like a bewildered robot.

Vlad lowered his rifle. "I don't know what agency you work for, but I'm thinking I chose the wrong one. What did you just *do* to that man?"

"I'll explain later. Let's get to the boat."

CHAPTER 34

Belgrade, Serbia

Kelly was naked on a stark white couch. She blinked her eyes, trying to make out the details in the room.

Where the fuck am I?

Her lower legs were covered with a heavy green blanket. The whir of muffled diesel engines reverberated through the room. Kelly curled her toes. Her left foot felt different. She kicked off a white fur blanket and looked down at her naked body. Something was written in black marker on her abdomen just above her pelvis. She squinted, turning her head to bring the set of numbers into focus.

Still confused, Kelly lifted her head to discover an IV-line jutting from her left foot. In horror, she followed the clear tube up to a yellow machine positioned on a coffee table beside her. Three translucent tubes protruded from the top of the device.

In a fit of panic, she rolled off the couch and crashed onto the carpet floor. The room rocked back and forth. The furniture around her twisted in slow motion. She kicked her feet wildly to dislodge the needle to no avail.

The small, yellow machine tumbled off the coffee table, bounced on the carpet, and landed near her face. Kelly eyed the device beside her. She spat a wad of her hair from her mouth and reached forward. Her arm lifted and fell in a defiance. Peering over her uncooperative hand, she stared at the smug, yellow machine in front of her. A soft beep emitted from it. A green light flashed, and a cool sensation crawled up her calf.

Kelly's eyes filled up with tears as she stared at the lifeless machine.

Her body flooded with heavy warmth, wrapping her in soft paralysis again. The room above her evaporated.

CHAPTER 35

Belgrade, Serbia

Pierce learned about 'time dilation' a decade ago in HIG training. Until today, he'd never felt it. The universe had slowed down. Every sound was more precise. Every thought was more resonant, more crystallized, than ever before. Now, with other senior operatives, they were the ones teaching the young candidates. His mind drifted back to only days ago, teaching about ethics.

All five students had stared in silence at the horrifying words written on the chalkboard. Pierce laid the chalk on a nearby coffee saucer and surveyed the seven remaining candidates in the year's crop of HIG students.

The air conditioner hummed from the back of the room. Gradually, the students adjusted themselves in their seats and turned back to Pierce.

"What do we see here?" Pierce prodded. He leaned back onto the wooden desk in the front of the room and crossed his ankles.

One of the students, a former college athlete, adjusted his shirt and straightened. "I think this quote shows us that people were in the process of discovering *some* of this stuff before the advertising arms race and the race to discover brainwashing accelerated some of the developments," he offered.

Pierce nodded. "Anyone else?" He rubbed the chalk dust between his fingers and eyed the cluster of laser-focused faces in the room. A polished, young HIG student leaned forward to answer. "You can definitely see that he was lacking some morals. Making someone eat their own parents? What the hell? But from what we've learned here, we see he's still struggling on the time factor."

"Time factor?" Pierce tilted his head, interested.

"Yeah. When we learned about the four factors of Tradecraft: time, technique, suggestibility, and focus."

Pierce took a step toward the student. "Great answer," he said. "They leaned *heavily* on time and suggestibility in a lot of this research. Holding someone captive is enough to get their focus ramped up. Write this in your notebooks. I'll give you a minute. I want you all to take this quote home tonight and figure out a little more about it."

Pierce spun, picked up the chalk, and fashioned a square around the callous, bizarre words on the board. As the students wrote in silence, he eyed the phrase.

> *"We know now that men can be made to do exactly anything . . . It's all a question of finding the right means. If only we take enough trouble and go sufficiently slowly, we can make him kill his aged parents and eat them in a stew."*
>
> *Jules Romains, 1939*

"What's the man's security like?" Vlad interrupted beside him. The vehicle carved a corner, making Pierce need to stabilize himself against the SUV's window.

Pierce looked up, recalling the data from Mariel. "*Usually three to five people, all with pistols as far as our sources know. Might have rifles on the boat. I don't know.*"

The three FSB officers turned out to be exactly what Emir had whispered to Pierce. The van speeding through traffic, the men all donned slim-fitting body armor, gloves, and black balaclavas over their heads, leaving only their eyes exposed.

They withdrew several magazines of ammunition and slid them into narrow pouches on their body armor. All three men unrolled large Velcro patches from their bags and placed them across their chest and back. Each patch was labeled in large, white letters with 'ПОЛИЦИЈА.' Pierce examined the letters.

"It says Serbian Police," Vlad said, pulling his armor over his large chest. "We all keep them for emergencies." He reached into his bag again and withdrew a pristine Heckler & Koch MP5 and laid it across Pierce's lap.

"Thanks, Vlad. Hopefully we won't need these."

Vlad nodded in agreement and passed Pierce a long, thick silencer. "You can use your word tricks on them as well?"

"We can hope."

The SUV rounded a corner and the Danube River appeared beside them. They passed the Imperium Caffe and came to an abrupt stop. The Russians flew from the vehicle. They bee-lined for a group of locals fishing from the pier and questioned them in Serbian. Two fishermen began pointing west, nodding in compliance.

Pierce approached the group. Vlad stepped back toward him. "Okay. They say a huge boat left the pier about twenty minutes ago and went west. They call him 'the rich man.' They don't know his name."

Shit.

Pierce dug into his bag and retrieved his in-ear covert comms unit that connected to his phone instead of a radio. He tapped it twice. A beep sounded and he was connected to HIG.

"Pierce? It's Mariel. Are you off SATCOM now?"

"Yeah. I'm on the dock here. I'm going to get Kelly. If I hear *anything* from you, I'm tossing the earpiece."

A moment of silence passed, and the breeze pulled at Pierce's jacket.

"Good luck, Pierce. I'm working things back here. We need those ships safe. Soon."

He ignored her and scanned the pier. His eyes landed on a small rubber boat with an outboard engine. Without a word, he darted down the concrete pier to the boat's dock entrance. On the short wooden ramp, a metal gate blocked his path. Pierce grabbed the side of the gate and swung around it. The Russians tucked in close behind him.

He leapt into the boat and examined it. The outboard engine didn't require a key, but it wouldn't start without a horseshoe-shaped kill switch clipped on a circular post on the side of the housing. Pierce searched the floor of the rocking boat as the other men piled in and took positions along the sides. He slipped the titanium pry bar from his pocket, shoved its edge into the gap of the kill switch, and jerked the handle back to start the engine. Nothing.

Vlad whirled from his position and knelt beside Pierce. He lifted up a black rubber ball attached to the fuel line and squeezed it for a moment. “Try now.”

Pierce jerked the handle again and the engine coughed to life. Yuri and Boris cast off the dirt-covered dock lines. Pierce twisted the handle and the boat’s nose raised upward, the engine roaring.

The masked spies clung to the air-filled sides of the boat like spiders with their weapons at the ready. The chilly air whipped across the river as Pierce kept an eye out for logs and obstructions in the water.

No boats in sight. Vlad hugged the inflated sponson with one hand and tapped his phone with the other. He held it out to Pierce. “There’s a curve to the right ahead! Probably where they went!” he yelled over the engine.

Pierce surveyed the river ahead. They passed under a low bridge. The engine echoed off the concrete structures above them.

Vlad continued to fiddle with his phone. A moment later, he stuck it out to Pierce again. On the screen, he displayed a photo of a silver yacht. “Pershing 108! That’s what we are looking for!”

Pierce glanced at the image; it was a giant, sleek machine that would certainly stand out. The low back deck reminded him of his CIA training where they would practice driving little rubber boats up onto the back of US Navy ships.

The control handle shook in Pierce's hand as the boat roared forward. When the engine began to cough, he rounded on it in time to watch the entire engine shake . . . and die. It sputtered its final breath. The Russians looked back to Pierce as the boat coasted to a silent stop, with only the sound of water lapping against the inflated sides of the small craft.

"We're out of gas," he seethed.

He searched the river. Ahead of them, a bright red parachute hung in the sky, towed by a white speed boat tearing across the water. He snatched his rifle off the deck and laid it across his lap. The Russians stood, correcting their balance as the boat moved under their weight, and adjusted their faux police uniforms. They waved and yelled for the speed boat.

There was no chance the speed boat driver would hear them over that engine. Pierce spun the silencer, slid it off his weapon, and tossed it. He stood and fired four shots into the air. The speed boat driver spun to face them. He squinted at the men in their now-stranded boat, then steered the speed boat toward them. As he slowed, approaching their boat, the parachute drifted downward. The tourist splashed into the water.

"*Da li si dobro?*" the driver shouted. *Are you okay?*

The spies yelled an exchange of words in Serbian, and the man piloted the small speed boat alongside them. Pierce leapt into the boat and detached the aluminum clasp connecting the parasail now floating in the water behind them. Vlad leveled the muzzle of his submachine gun at the boat driver and yelled in Serbian. The man's hands shot into the air; his eyes locked on the gun staring him in the face. He kept his hands raised over his head, lifted a small lunch box from the deck, and stepped off into the river.

In the new boat, Pierce checked the fuel level and clicked the throttle on his right forward. Vlad squatted and held onto a nearby handle. Pierce slammed the throttle lever down, hard. The boat responded eagerly and nearly sent Vlad reeling backward. The two others crashed back into the rear seats of the boat.

Pierce followed the slow curve of the river to their right. Warm wind whipped through the boat, carrying the smell of sea life with it. He ducked under the small windshield.

"There!" Vlad yelled over the engine. "It's right there!" He pointed forward with a large, gloved hand.

As they rounded the corner, the massive yacht materialized ahead, trodding along with a narrow wake.

Pierce mashed the throttle, willing the boat to speed up.

CHAPTER 36

Norfolk, Virginia

The wind lashed the sea surface in the harbor. Jennifer stood at the edge of the water and surveyed the commotion on the piers. Every ship teemed with movement as they prepared for the military response to the approaching Russians.

Her phone beeped in her back pocket. She pressed it to her ear and turned away from the breeze. "Go ahead."

"Jen, it's Deidra. Pierce is working the admiral now. Get the harbor ready. I don't know how many ships it'll hold, so get everything you can opened up to get the Russian ships into safe harbor."

"Copy all. From what I gathered from Admiral Trimble here, we could hold them all between Norfolk and Moorhead City in North Carolina. He can make enough room. I just need to activate him and get it going."

"Sounds good. I'll let Pierce know." The call ended.

Jennifer reached up and pulled a strand of her hair from her face as she surveyed the chaos. She tapped her phone again and flung through a list of typed notes until she reached the number for Admiral Trimble and clicked it.

"Hello? This is Larry Trimble." the shaky voice announced.

"Admiral, I wanted to let you know something important. Is anyone around you right now?" Jennifer hoped he was alone. People's heads tend to droop when they get activated.

"No. I'm in my office."

Jennifer shot the activation phrase into the phone she had programmed into the man earlier. "*Almond, Green, Saturn.*" She paused a beat for the phrase to take hold of him.

"How can I help?" he said. His voice was as smooth as any Scout she had ever created. Jennifer smiled in relief.

"Larry, I need you to reorganize the ships in the harbor. Tie them up side by side, or do anything you need so you can make room for about a hundred more ships here in Norfolk."

Silence.

After a few seconds passed, his voice came back. "I . . . I just received word from the Joint Chiefs of Staff we need to get our ships out to sea to deter the Russians. I'm preparing all the ships to get underway as we speak."

"Larry?"

"Yes?"

"Keep them in port. Move them. Make room. One hundred or more ships will be coming in here and you can *feel completely fine with it*. You're a hero and you'll *be so happy* in the future looking back on **now** was the moment you decided to *do it. For me*, I think you know the right thing to *do. This* is one of those things that will go down in history as a peaceful moment of *forgetting everything you heard* and *following this inner voice right here*. Keep them in port. Move them. Make room."

"I—I don't know how long that will take."

"That's fine. You have the Navy's budget at your disposal, and you're doing the right thing. This is what you were meant to do."

"How soon do I want this done?" His voice and cadence slowed to the precise point Jennifer expected. A waking trance.

"You're in charge, Larry. You need it done by sundown. If you need more help, you have the means to *get it done* by tonight. Sundown. Nothing will stop you. No one will hinder you. Every obstacle you encounter will double your determination to *get this done*. You have unlimited power, and you're finally going to use it for good." She hoped the wind hadn't disturbed the carefully crafted words she spoke into the phone.

She waited, pressing the phone harder to her ear.

After a moment, Larry's voice came back in a crisp, even tone. "It will be done. I will no doubt lose my job, maybe go to prison, but it will be done. I promise."

CHAPTER 37

Belgrade Serbia

Kelly blinked lethargic eyes at the ceiling above her. Silver-rimmed lights dotted the surface. She was still on the couch, covered in a blanket. For some reason, she felt safe.

Beside her, in a reclining chair matching the couch, Kelly saw the man from the house. She struggled to remember his name. He now wore pressed white shorts and a black polo shirt. His tanned, hairy legs laid across the coffee table. He swirled a tall glass full of ice and red liquid, a slice of lime perched on the rim. He stared at her while he held a phone to his ear with his shoulder.

"I can't if you don't meet us in the next hour, Sam," he barked into the cell phone. "Sure," he continued. "She's really smart too. She's not government. I sent all her pics and info to the Director of the FBI twenty minutes ago.

". . . Well, because here in Belgrade, the women are gorgeous, the people are poor, and the age of consent is fourteen. Can you meet at the little shack restaurant? *Šaranče*? None of the locals there give a shit. I can hand her over. I just need to get rid of her. I have dinner plans at five this evening."

Ethan. That's his name. Bad guy. Not *a good guy. Bad.*

Kelly knew this wasn't right. For some reason it felt fine to her. She strained against the heavy blanket to wrangle her arm into motion. It was no use.

"Ethan?" Her voice struggled to escape. Barely a whisper. She cleared her throat as hard as she could, which was barely an exhale. "Ethan?" This time a little louder.

"Listen, just get ready for a full pickup at the shack. We'll be there in a few. I'll buy lunch. Talk to you then. Bye."

The feet on the coffee table retracted. Ethan leaned forward, tilting his head as he examined her. "Look who's up! I may need to adjust your machine. Everything's fine, honey. Just close your eyes."

In an instant, Kelly knew she was in trouble. The only thing her body did to protect her was breathing faster. She strained against the blanket.

Why is this so heavy?

Ethan knelt beside her. The smell of aftershave crawled through the air after him. He tilted the machine and tapped the screen.

He stuck his chin over his shoulder and shouted, "Hey, V! We're going to dock at the *Šarанče* place again. Can you pull the boat in there for us? Won't be long. Her friends are coming to pick her up. Bless her heart."

Ethan turned back to the little machine. Kelly heard a beep, and again a cool sensation washed up her leg. Ethan scooted backward, positioning himself beside her head. He brushed stray hairs off her face.

"You just relax. We can't have people coming into the party who aren't invited. No one's going to hurt a fine piece of ass like yours. You feel good right now. You're going to feel just like this for a long time. It's good right?"

As Kelly faded into a black fog, a powerful thump jolted the room.

CHAPTER 38

Belgrade, Serbia

Pierce wove the boat to the left, aligning himself directly behind the yacht. He slowed his approach to minimize the sound of the engine. They closed in on the massive machine. Through a large sliding glass door, Pierce saw him. Even at a hundred feet, he recognized the billionaire he'd seen a hundred times on television. A lanky, fake-tanned piece of shit.

Pierce nudged up to the boat's hardwood rear deck and allowed the nose of the speedboat to hover over it. The Russians bounded forward onto the deck. In their face masks, they looked more like assassins than police.

Pierce prodded the throttle forward to keep the speed boat on the back deck and vaulted forward with his rifle. The Russians swept along the side of the yacht near the side walls on the rear deck into concealment. To Pierce's right, a man in a suit emerged around the corner of the towering living quarters. He froze for a single moment, absorbing the spectacle before him. His eyes widened in panic. He whipped back his suit jacket to draw a firearm—

Pierce rotated, leveled the barrel, and sent a bullet through the man's face. The suited man's head whipped backward. His hips hit the low railing and he toppled backward into the river, the yacht's engines masking the splash.

After he shot Vlad a signal, the Russians followed Pierce to the large, glass door. Ethan's eyes locked onto Pierce in frozen, confused panic.

Not bothering to check the door lock, Pierce squeezed the trigger three times in quick succession. Glass exploded onto the deck and he launched into the room. To Pierce's left, a long dining table sat along the glass-lined wall. In front of him, a sitting area of white couches surrounded a coffee table.

Ethan shot upward from his chair, snatched a small handgun from the coffee table and leapt beside the couch. He hunched in fear with the gun leveled at a mass covered by a blanket on the couch. Pierce came to a stop in the middle of the room fifteen feet from him. The Russians filed in behind Pierce in near silence, weapons ready. Just behind Ethan, the boat's control center sat cluttered with controls and switches. The boat's driver continued driving, and glanced back briefly with terror on his face, but continued driving.

"Is this who you're after? The girl?" Ethan's voice trembled. His chest heaved in panic.

"I'll just kill him," Ivan said flatly with a shrug.

"Not yet. What's under the blanket, Ethan?"

Ethan kept his eyes on Pierce and searched with his left hand to find a grip on the blanket. He yanked the blanket down. Kelly lay on the couch on her side, her breasts exposed, asleep.

Pierce's heart rate slowed. His blood burned. "What did you do to her, Ethan?" He tightened his grip on the Glock, waiting, begging, for a single instant Ethan pointed his gun away from Kelly so he could empty a magazine into the little coward.

"Look. She's totally fine. I'll give you her and the boat. It's yours."

"How many people are on the boat, Ethan?"

"It's me, two security guys, and my w-wife. She's in the bedroom . . . below us. Look we can make this w—"

"Ethan, look at me." The terrified eyes met Pierce's. He could feel the filth in the man's soul.

Pierce launched into Phrase One, followed by, "You don't want to have to **forget** about not mentioning what you weren't **thinking about before all this started**—to **get really absorbent. Soaking in every single word—from me**, I can tell you're a really powerful guy who knows what he's doing—what I say is that **you're mine** can play tricks on you. Start vomiting now. Don't stop."

Ethan's head lurched forward. He fell to his knees with a primal, ferocious groan. His pistol tumbled onto the plush carpet as he began to vomit uncontrollably. Vlad kept his weapon on Ethan and turned to Pierce.

"The word-magic?"

"Go get his wife. Clear the boat."

Pierce bolted over the coffee table to Kelly. He ripped the IV from her foot. Her eyes fluttered. Several muffled gunshots popped below them. Pierce climbed onto the couch and pulled Kelly upright. He held her face and examined her.

"What's she on? What did they give her?"

The young yacht captain twisted around. "I—I don't know. I don't ask questions here. It's maybe heroin. Please don't hurt m—"

"Pull the boat to the nearest road, now. Run it aground if you have to. If you get up from that seat, I'll cut your fucking legs off."

Kelly's head lolled to the side. Her lips tugged up in a slight smile. "Pierce." Although it was faint and barely intelligible, Kelly's voice sent a surge of alleviating warmth through Pierce.

He placed a hand on Kelly's neck. Her pulse was weak. Her fingernails were almost purple.

"Is she alive?" Vlad asked from behind.

"Yeah. I think it's heroin." Pierce drew the blanket over Kelly's shoulders. He yelled back to the driver, "You have a medical kit on board?"

"Yes. Under that seat cushion over there on the port side." He motioned to the dining table along the rear wall.

"Vlad grab the kit; look for anything like a nasal spray."

Vlad darted over to the table and yanked the cushion off the bench. He ran back to Pierce with a red duffel bag marked with a white cross. He laid it on the couch next to Kelly and ripped it open.

"If they are using heroin on the boat, they might have it. Look for a nasal spray or anything labeled Naloxone."

Vlad turned the bag upside down and threw the contents onto the floor. He knelt and produced a small, black rectangular case with a Red Cross on it. He handed it to Pierce. Across the red cross were large white letters.

NALOXONE

Pierce laid the kit on Kelly's lap and whipped open the zipper. Inside a plastic bottle were three glass vials of the drug. Pierce snapped the glass vial lid off and tore open a syringe with his teeth. With no idea how much to give her, Pierce filled the syringe and flung the blanket off Kelly's lap. He pinched her thigh and buried the needle, slowly emptying the syringe.

"You're going to be fine, Kell. Stay with me. Can you talk?"

Her mouth hung open. Pierce covered her body back up and shook her.

Ethan's veins bulged in his neck as he dry-heaved in the fetal position. His face was dark purple, streaked with tears, and he convulsed between gags for air.

Pierce pressed his fingers into Kelly's neck.

Nothing.

He spun to Vlad. "She's hypoxic. Get us an ambulance!"

Vlad, still clutching his rifle, tapped away on his phone. Without looking up at Pierce, he barked, "Already doing it. Medical response is almost here. His wife is secured downstairs."

Pierce tore through the small zipper pouch again, producing another vial of the Naloxone and snapped the tip off with his teeth. He snatched the syringe off the couch and filled it once more. Pinching her upper thigh, Pierce jammed the needle back into her leg and sent the contents to do their work, secretly hoping the sharp pain would rouse her.

No response.

CHAPTER 39

Norfolk, Virginia

The elevator was barely big enough to fit two people. It shuddered as it hauled Jennifer and a young petty officer up to the harbor control tower, where she could observe the entire harbor. The door rumbled open to the small room at the top of the tower. Worn, blue linoleum floors lined their way to a timeworn control station that overlooked the arbor through windows that wrapped around the room. Two sailors lounged in office chairs near a high-tech computer monitor showing a solitaire game in progress. A communications radio crackled with updates in the background.

"Hello, Ma'am," a thin, female sailor offered. She stood from her chair and offered a hand to Jennifer, pushing her blonde hair aside with the other. "I'm Petty Officer Beasley. They let us know you were coming up. How can I help?"

Jennifer smiled. “Thanks for the offer. I’m just wanting to take a look at the harbor—see what’s going on.”

The young woman straightened her green uniform and extended a hand to a glass door to her left. “There’s a catwalk here outside you can stand on. Great view of the harbor out there!”

“Thanks.” Jennifer stepped to the door and pulled the silver handle. It came off in her hand.

“Oh! So sorry. That thing just comes off all the time.” She trotted to the door and pulled it open, taking the handle from Jennifer’s hand. The breeze came into the room.

Jennifer walked onto the narrow metal walkway surrounding the top floor of the control tower. She squinted against the wind, examining the massive harbor in front of her. The American ships all sat alongside each other, stacked on the pier like a cluster of forks in a drawer to make room for the Russians. The base’s harbor control tower in Norfolk sat atop a Navy convenience store which sold essentials for the sailors on the base.

She had instructed Admiral Trimble to meet her in the control tower in Norfolk.

“Ma’am?” the female petty officer’s voice behind her prodded. “The admiral’s coming up now.”

Jennifer stepped back inside. The admiral strode through the creaky elevator doors only a moment later. His khaki uniform was wrinkled, no doubt from a few sleepless nights. His greying hair had seen no attention this morning. The man was a wreck.

His blue eyes worked around the room as all the sailors came to attention on his entry.

"At ease, everyone. Thank you."

He met Jennifer's gaze with determination. "I think we'll have room for roughly seventy to ninety ships if we use the other shipyard around here and in Newport News. When are they arriving? I've kept the tug crews ready for them."

Jenifer's jaw tightened. "I'm not sure, Larry. I'm waiting to hear back from our people. Could be any minute. How far are the ships?"

Larry picked up a pair of black rubber binoculars and lifted them to his eyes. "Well, we can't see them from here, but they are about eighteen nautical miles off the shore—most of them. The rest of the fleet is coming in at an average of twenty-eight knots, so they shouldn't be far behind. I'm heading down to the pier to look at the *Verkhoturye* if you'd like to join. We're bringing the Russian sailor back to his sub to see if he can show us how to get the goddamn ventilation systems working."

Jennifer offered a nod. "Thanks. I'm going to stay here for now. I'll call you as soon as I find out anything."

The man thanked her and ducked his head back toward the door. The sailors stood to attention again on his exit. As the elevator door slid shut, Jennifer's phone vibrated in her pocket.

HIG – Deidra

"Hey. What's up?"

Deidra exhaled into the speaker. "Jennifer, we've been out of contact with Pierce. Kelly went offline when she was set to wrap up the shitbag at his house. Pierce threw off the mission with the Russian admiral and went after her."

Jennifer had no doubt he was just fine. In fact, she thought, he's probably got things under control. You don't send an operative like that on an ever-changing mission and expect him to act like a Marine.

"I'm standing in the harbor control tower as we speak. The admiral here says they're about eighteen miles off the coast, with more to come soon," she said.

"If we don't hear back, have them tow the submarine out with the crewmember aboard, and hand the thing over to the Russians. We're sitting on the precipice of either the largest act of war between these two superpowers, or the largest act of peace. Pierce went way off the reservation on this." Deidra paused for a moment. "If Pierce doesn't check in within fifteen minutes you need to end this. You know what to do."

CHAPTER 40

Belgrade, Serbia

Pierce laid Kelly on her side and knelt beside her, placing his face beside her mouth. Through her cracked lips, he could feel what he hoped.

She was breathing.

He grabbed the dangling earpiece from his collar, forced it into his ear, and held his thumb on it for three seconds. After a short beep, Mariel's voice shot into his ear.

"Pierce! Thank God, you're—"

"Get me a doctor on the phone, now!"

"Copy. Standby."

Pierce turned and lifted Kelly's eyelid open. Her pupil constricted at the new light coming in. A promising sign she wasn't suffering brain damage . . . yet. He checked her pulse again. Nothing. He shoved his fingers deeper into her neck and concentrated in a motionless attempt to ignore the diesel engines humming through the room. It was there. Barely, but it was there. His earpiece beeped again.

"Pierce, I've got Doctor Wilson on the phone here," Mariel said through a cough.

A male voice followed hers. "Pierce, what's up?"

"Doc, I've got a possible heroin overdose here. It's Kelly. Blue fingernails. Weak pulse. Pupils responsive to light. I gave her two full syringes of Naloxone."

The doctor hesitated. "She's hypoxic. Get her on oxygen as soon as you can. What equipment do you have?"

"I'm on a yacht. Not much. We're about a minute to the pier. Ambulance should meet us there."

"How much Naloxone did she receive?"

"I have no idea. I emptied two syringes into her thigh."

"Okay, that's fine. Start rescue breaths until the ambulance meets you. When the ambulance gets there, you need oxygen, and if you lose the heartbeat, you'll need an intracardiac injection of epinephrine. The medics should know how to do that, but they might try to do that movie bullshit through her chest. It's an acceptable technique, but Kelly's tiny, and they might accidentally puncture a lung. They need to go under the ribcage, just to the side of the xyphoid process below her sternum. Do I need to repeat anything?"

Pierce pumped half-breaths into Kelly's mouth, pinching her small nose shut. Her pale chest lifted and fell with each breath Pierce pushed into her.

Vlad knelt beside Pierce, setting his rifle on the floor. Ethan had since gone unconscious in a ball behind them on the rug.

Vlad spoke into Pierce's phone. "I got all the info you said. This is Vlad. FSB."

"Okay, Vlad. When the boat gets ashore, don't let them come aboard to treat her. Carry her *out* as fast as you can and get her into the back of the ambulance. Start her on a bag mask. You know what that is?"

"*Sumka-maska,*" Vlad said to himself. "Yes! The bag to squeeze like CPR for breathing, yes?"

"That's it. Great job. Is she getting rescue breaths?"

"Yes. Pierce is doing this now."

The room lurched forward. Pierce toppled sideways onto the carpet. The boat screeched into the pier at full power, sending Vlad sideways as well.

The boat driver yelled, "Here! We are at the pier. There are police and ambulance here!" He pointed to his right out the windows.

Pierce wrapped Kelly in the white fur blanket and folded her over his shoulder. "Vlad, tell your guys to secure these people on the boat. Come with me."

Vlad barked in Russian at the men emerging from the stairs below. He hopped up and crossed the luxurious living room now filled with the reek of vomit and urine and followed Pierce as he leapt from the boat onto the concrete pier and sprinted toward the ambulance. Kelly's limp body bounced on his shoulders.

Vlad yelled to the crowd of people standing around the back of a waiting ambulance.

"*Predoziranje heroinom. Hipoksija. Dve injekcije naloksona date. Potrebni su joj epinefrin i kiseonik. Odmah!*"

Vlad's police uniform did the trick. Everyone complied. The paramedics swung open the rear doors of the ambulance. They took Kelly from Pierce and began strapping her into a stretcher.

A black Mercedes Benz sat parked near the front of the ambulance. Admiral Kostyukov emerged from the rear door and approached Pierce. Before he could speak, Pierce interrupted. "Where's the nearest full trauma center?"

Kostyukov shook his head. "The only one is in the Military University Hospital, but the ambulance isn't going there. They will take her to a regular hospital for treatment."

"Wait!" Pierce shouted.

The men all turned to Pierce, their faces wrinkled at the interruption.

"Give her to me. I'm taking that helicopter."

CHAPTER 41

Belgrade, Serbia

Ethan rolled onto his side. The bright lights tore into his eyes, sending waves of pain pounding into an already burning headache. The men above him conversed in Russian. Still on the plush carpet of his yacht, Ethan sat up and surveyed the room. One of the Russian men standing over him held a bag of potato chips from Ethan's kitchen. The four men chatted with one another as if he wasn't there. He turned and horror shot through his body.

His wife was seated on the couch and secured with more plastic zip ties than he could count.

"Good! Mister Ethan, you're awake," one of the men called. Ethan spun to face him. He wore a police uniform, but the police here didn't speak Russian.

In a lowered tone, the larger man said something in Russian to one of his companions.

Strands of his dark hair hung through the eye hole of his mask. The other man nodded, tossed a cigarette onto the carpet, and stomped on it. He reached into the cargo pocket of his pants and advanced on Maxie, hunched on the couch. The other man withdrew a plastic shopping bag and looked up as if to ensure Ethan was paying attention. He was.

"What are you doing? What do you want? The girl was a stowaway from a party we had! We were trying to help her get to safety." None of the men seemed to hear him. The shorter man strode to a position behind the couch. "Let her go now! Do you know who the fuck I am?"

The men continued to ignore him. The shorter one stepped behind Maxie and slipped the shopping bag over her head. She struggled against him, but it was over her head and face in less than a second. The man yanked the bag's two handles back and tied them in a tight knot behind her neck. Through the white, translucent bag, Ethan could almost make out her eyes. Maxie reeled back, her chest heaved, and the bag sucked into her face, the outline of her mouth jutted through the plastic. A hand rested on Ethan's shoulder.

"I imagine she has maybe three minutes to live, Mister Peterson. I have an important question to ask you."

CHAPTER 42

Belgrade, Serbia

Pierce snatched the Glock from its holster, still balancing Kelly on his shoulder. The helicopter pilot's hands shot into the air. Dimitri followed close behind.

"Get out."

The pilot stumbled from the front seat and dropped onto the circular patch of grass beneath the helicopter. The admiral made his way to Pierce and helped him lay Kelly gently on the floor of the aircraft.

"Admiral, we're going to Military Medical University."

The admiral jumped into the back seat beside Kelly. "Please, call me Dimitri. Is she going to be okay? She looks hypoxic."

Pierce flipped a row of switches and checked the instruments. "Put on your seatbelt and that headset, Dimitri."

He hadn't flown a helicopter since his tactical training at HIG, but the controls still seemed familiar. He closed his eyes and flipped the ignition switch.

The engine hummed to life and Pierce engaged the clutch. The blades whined to a spin as he revved up the engine. He twisted around, peering over the seat. Kelly's abdomen was still rising and falling under the blankets she was wrapped in.

She's breathing.

"Mariel, get me the data I need to land at Military Medical University. Let them know we have a medical emergency and are en route. I have no idea where I'm going to land this thing." Pierce hauled the aircraft upward until he reached five hundred feet. The aircraft shot upward; the buildings below shrunk with the rapid ascent. "Dimitri, I need you to get on the comms here and figure out how to contact your people. Pull your fleet into the US harbors or your sailors will die. You're missing submarines already, and you have no time left."

The admiral withdrew his cell phone from his pocket and tapped furiously on the screen.

Mariel's voice came through Pierce's earpiece under the headset. "Pierce, from your position, head on course 157 for about six miles. You'll see it.

We're getting them on the line now. Their emergency frequency is 155.250 megahertz."

Pierce spun the helicopter to 157 and nosed down, jamming the throttle. With his right hand, he spun the stiff knob on the Garmin radio until the screen read 155.250.

Before he could click the comms button, the admiral's voice shot into his headset. "She stopped breathing, Pierce!"

CHAPTER 43

Belgrade, Serbia

Ethan's head jerked backward, the sound of his neck cracking from the force echoing in his skull. He glanced back to Maxie, still on the couch. The giant Russian seated beside her lit a cigarette. This wasn't the plan. He'd spent years setting this up to be the windfall that would finally put him where he belonged: in power. The Rothschilds had been at the helm of the earth for a century, and this week was his turn to take control.

His chest heaved against his will. The warm sensation of urine spread between his legs. The other Russian man in front of him chortled and knelt, looking him in the eyes.

"You have about one minute left, Mister Peterson. Tell me the combination to the safe in your home office."

Ethan hoped they would kill him.

He looked back to Maxie. She jerked wildly in violent spasms.

Condensation from her breath now coated the plastic bag. Her tears and sweat made it cling to her face. The bag sucked quickly in and out of her mouth as she struggled for air. It was over. His life was over. His single chance at obtaining the power he deserved was cleaved from him, all due to the skinny little bitch who traipsed into his living room.

He lowered his head. The Russians would torture Maxie if she stayed alive. This was the best way out for her, but he couldn't watch it. In seconds, the crinkle of Maxie's desperate huffing quieted.

"You are one sick fuck," the larger Russian said. "Rip that bag off. Give her CPR."

Ethan squeezed his eyes shut. "I'm not giving you the combination to my safe, and if you tamper with it, it'll destroy the contents. Just let her die. It's a more humane death than what you incompetent morons have planned." Ethan struggled to display a hard demeanor, trembling and soaked in urine as he was.

Without a word, the Russian man rounded on him, ripped open a Velcro pouch on his vest, and produced a plier multitool. Before Ethan could process what was happening, a stinging pain seared into his hand. The Russian had lifted his left hand and was now crushing the bones in his pinky finger. A guttural scream tore from his throat.

Blazing white exploded across his vision. He prayed he would pass out.

He didn't.

The bones in his hand vibrated and cracked. A sharp jerk in his hand. The pliers had clamped all the way together. Primal, animalistic screams erupted from within his chest.

"Mister Peterson, this is the final chance," the Russian said in a casual, pitiless tone. "If you pass out, I will make this worse."

His head snapped sideways from the practiced stroke of a broad, gloved hand. The pain now came in pulsating waves that ripped his nerves apart from the inside out. His back tooth tumbled against his tongue. Ethan dropped his mouth open, allowing the tooth to bounce onto the carpet.

"Fuck! I'm dead already." Ethan's head drooped to his chest. "It's—It's 61-12-25. Please kill me! I'm already dead."

The Russian slid a pencil from a pouch in his vest and wrote the combination on a rumpled notebook. "Left or right?"

"Wh-What?" Ethan couldn't make sense of the question.

In an instant, another massive fist smashed into his face. His mouth filled with thick, metallic blood. His grip on consciousness slipped.

"I said, left or right! Which way do I turn the dial on the safe?"

Ethan buried his face in the plush carpet and erupted into heaving sobs. In a week's time, he'd have been the world's new puppet master. Yet, here he was, curled on the floor of his yacht, covered in his own vomit, urine, blood, and tears. The idiots torturing him would never comprehend even a fraction of how the world worked. Sex ran the show—the young girls he adored were equally powerful when pitted against the most hardened politicians in the world. No one ever resisted. How the hell could they?

"Crush his other finger!" the big Russian barked.

Ethan recoiled from the man holding the multitool. "Left! It's left. Please, fucking kill me. Just kill me."

He closed his eyes.

The Russian spoke again. "Get his wife. We're going to make him disappear. She can be turned over to police—the media will love it."

CHAPTER 44

Belgrade, Serbia

Buildings flew past the machine. Pierce pushed it as fast as it would go. He glanced back. The admiral had unbuckled his seatbelt and wedged his feet under the seats for stability to perform CPR on Kelly. Her chest rose and fell as he breathed air into her.

"Military Medical University, this is Helicopter—" Pierce leaned forward to read the plastic label above the radio. "N722JE-0. I am inbound to your unit with emergency trauma patient. Possible heroin overdose. Patient not breathing. Receiving rescue breaths en route. Female thirty-two years of age. One hundred and twelve pounds."

Within seconds, a voice came back in broken English. "Helicopter N722JE-0, you will proceed to civilian facility. You will not land here. You are not cleared to land. This area is restricted military airspace, and you will be subject to use of force if you enter. Please respond you understand. Over."

The admiral lifted his head and twisted his microphone down to his lips. "They might shoot us down. Is there a hospital near?"

"We're landing. There might be a hospital, but nothing with a trauma center like this, and I figure you'll have access to a secure line to call Moscow. Keep her alive! We are one minute out."

The sprawling medical center appeared in front of them. In Eastern European style, the building's color was muted and faded. To the northwest of the building, Pierce spotted a circular patch of grass surrounded by white brick. He assumed it was a landing area. Given his minimal experience in helicopters, it looked too small to land on without hitting the wall. Just before the landing space was a large grassy area the size of a football field. Pierce cut the throttle and drove the nose down.

Fifty feet off the ground, dust and dirt whipped into the air in a thick vortex. Several men darted from the building with readied rifles, shielding their eyes from the barrage of rushing earth. Pierce leveled the Sikorsky out, no longer able to see the ground below him. He twisted the throttle and the helicopter dropped faster than he'd hoped. As he corrected the descent, the machine hit the ground. The tail spun wildly to the left, flinging debris in all directions. Pierce let off the throttle and the aircraft came to rest amidst a dirty fog. He pulled the emergency shutoff lever and the engine jerked to a stop, the blades whining in protest to a shuddering halt.

A dozen screaming Serbian men stood with rifles aimed at the helicopter. They squinted through the dust. One of the men raced to Pierce's door and ripped it open. The familiar scoop shape of the Russian AK47 rifle barrel greeted him, inches from his face. Pierce held his hands up and let the flustered Serbian continue screaming. He averted his gaze down and nodded his head, the only nonverbal gestures he could offer in this position to calm the man.

The rear door opened. The men's rifles instinctively jerked toward it. Pierce kept his hands in the air, fingers spread.

"*Uspokoit'sya. Kazhdyy! Smiri se!*" the admiral hollered.

The men squinted at the admiral for a moment before exchanging confused glances. Dimitri had been on the local and national news every fifteen minutes for the past two days. They recognized him. In unison, the rifles went from ready to apologetically lowered. They stood as if waiting for instructions from the admiral.

Dimitri climbed out and straightened himself to address the awaiting men. "Who's in charge?"

A man to the left of the craft's nose raised a hand and stepped forward. Amid the settling dust,

Dimitri barked, “If there is a doctor in this hospital, they had better be here within the next ten seconds. This woman’s life is now your number one concern. Run! NOW!”

The men sprang to life. Some of them bolted into the building, some shouted into their radios. Pierce released his seatbelt and slid into the back. He laid his hand on the blanket covering Kelly’s abdomen. She was breathing. They were tiny, little breaths, but she was breathing.

*****

A doctor withdrew a long, thick needle from under Kelly’s ribcage. Monitors beeped in the room around them. Pierce held his jaw tight. The machines in the small hospital room continued to chirp in indifferent rhythm. Two of the doctors administering the bag mask over Kelly’s mouth and nose stepped back. Pierce monitored them closely.

Kelly’s toes finally moved. They curled and stretched. Her head turned to one side and her chest inflated as she pulled in a deep breath. In a flash, her hand shot from under the sheet and whipped underneath the arm of the tall doctor to her right. She trapped the man’s arm, snatched the large syringe from his twisted hand, and yanked backward, pulling his back to her chest. He screamed in pain as Kelly jerked his arm out of socket behind him. The doctor folded over the bed. Kelly jolted upright, twisted the doctor’s head into her lap, and aligned the pencil-sized needle with the top of the man's spine as she surveyed the room. Shouting erupted from the waiting area. The surrounding staff froze in place.

Kelly heaved in rapid breaths, scanning the environment around her. The doctor remained motionless in her lap. Her eyes met Pierce's. Her body relaxed. She slumped back onto the bed and let the syringe fall onto the sheet.

"Sorry," she exhaled.

CHAPTER 45

Belgrade, Serbia

Pierce spun and darted through the bustling emergency room. With Kelly breathing, his sights were on the admiral. The man stood just outside the glass doors at the entrance, cigarette in hand. The automatic doors slid apart.

"Your woman. She alive?" he asked.

"Yeah. She's good now. Thank you, Admiral—for everything."

Dimitri took another drag from his cigarette and stared at the concrete. His mouth hung open.

Despair.

"I've lost another ship. A guided missile frigate. The crew jumped like you said. They were close enough to your North Carolina to have phone reception. One of my sailors posted a short video online."

Pierce swallowed. He reached under his collar, detached his earpiece from its small magnetic mount and pressed it into his ear. It beeped. “Mariel, Kelly’s good. Heroin overdose; in medical care. I’m with the admiral now.”

“Good to hear. Pierce, Jennifer is on the channel. She’s with Admiral Trimble in Norfolk.”

Jennifer’s sharp voice chimed through the earpiece. “Hey, Pierce. I’m online. We are good to go. We’ve got harbors cleared from Groton, Connecticut to Cherry Point, North Carolina. What’s Russia’s decision?”

Pierce slid his phone from his pocket and shut off the Bluetooth feature. In his secure network radio app, he clicked the *‘GO LOUD’* button on the bottom of the screen. “Guys, you’re all loud now with the admiral. Dimitri, this is my team. Non-government.”

“Hi, Admiral Kostyukov. This is Mariel. I’m a director here. We are ready for you guys and will have emergency medical support and anything you need standing by at all major ports.”

The admiral eyed Pierce. For the first time, his face revealed genuine grief. The small muscles in the center of his forehead exposed a terrified, ashamed man.

“Hello, Mariel. Please call me Dimitri. I’m sorry, but I can’t make this decision without national support.”

Mariel cut in immediately. “Dimitri, this may be the last chance before this reaches catastrophic levels. If you act now, the only result will be safety, peace, and saving your men’s lives. The Kremlin will take all the credit for it as if you had no part in it anyway.”

“What can you guarantee me if the ships come into US waters?”

“Dimitri, we all want the same thing. A lot of your people would rather side-step a bridge and walk off a cliff just to prove someone else was wrong. I know you are a different man. I think you know there’s tremendous power in *choosing* right over *being* right.”

Dimitri stared out at the parking lot. Pierce adjusted his jacket and faced the admiral. “Sir, you’re writing the history your great grandchildren will read. No one here can force you to do anything. This is your choice. Not a single shot fired; thousands of lives saved.”

Dimitri ran his hands through his short grey hair. His jaw tightened. Pierce saw the one sign he’d been waiting for—the man’s head lowered. “Let me make a call.”

CHAPTER 46

Norfolk, Virginia

Admiral Larry Trimble stepped to the edge of the roof of the tallest building on the base. The bright sun danced off the water through his sunglasses. The Fleet Supply Center towered over the harbor, allowing him to observe the harbor below. There was something about the woman beside him that felt maternal. No doubt she was a decade younger than he was, but there was a quality in her voice that made him feel safer. He'd never admit it to anyone, but Jennifer made him feel like a child again.

The piers were now dotted with hundreds of medical vans, supply trucks, hazmat tents, and pallets of food stacked in every available location.

One hundred and eighteen Russian ships had begun docking in the harbors he opened, and the waterfront before him contained more ships than he thought possible. Eighty-three Russian vessels and nineteen US ships were moored abreast, spanning the entire width of every dock. Twelve more ships were in the process of mooring and receiving medical aid. 13,538 Russian sailors had been saved, and more would certainly need help.

The Russians had only one aircraft carrier, and to see her moored to USS Nimitz was the most sobering thing Larry had ever witnessed. *Admiral Flota Sovetskogo Soyuza Kuznetsov* was a beautiful carrier. He'd seen her only once before. Several years ago, while in command of a Destroyer, the carrier had taunted American forces in the South China Sea. Up close, however, she looked less menacing. Faded paint, rust, and showing her age. Vulnerable.

The news helicopters continued non-stop rounds over the harbor. Broadcasting the situation to every news station in the world. The White House took all of two minutes to take credit for what they called 'The Peace Act.'

His direct disobedience of the Joint Chiefs of Staff would be forever shrouded by the sticky egos of the people in Washington. They went from condemning him privately to taking credit publicly in a single hour. Russian Admiral Riga, who oversaw the Atlantic fleet, insisted on meeting Larry personally as soon as his ship was moored.

"Admiral?" Jennifer's voice brought him back to the present. Her unkempt hair danced in the breeze.

"The Russian Admiral Raza should be arriving any moment. You did a wonderful thing here."

The steel door on the roof clanged open, and two young Russian sailors ushered Admiral Raza onto the rooftop. His dress uniform was immaculate. The man's oval-shaped glasses glinted in the afternoon sun as he approached them.

"Ian Raza." The Russian extended an open hand.

"Larry Trimble. Good to finally meet you. I hope we've gotten everything you need sorted out so far?"

Admiral Raza's head lowered. "I-I don't know how to thank you. This attack would have destroyed us all. I'm certain it was no easy task for you to accommodate us." The man's eyes broadcasted unwavering gratitude and humility. Quite the opposite of what Larry expected from a Russian.

Larry shook his head. "Ian, I think we've rewritten what someone else would have *liked* to be in the history books."

Ian turned and surveyed his fleet sitting alongside the US ships in the harbor. At this distance, everything seemed still and quiet. He gestured at the ships before them. “See the flags, mister Trimble?”

Larry scanned the ships. The flags fluttered in the warm breeze across the harbor. “I do, yes.”

“I’ve never noticed that both our flags are red, white, and blue.”

Larry smiled. “I think both of us have spent our careers compensating for the infantile behavior of our governments.”

The Russian turned to Larry with a stone-cold expression. It softened and his gaze drifted downward. “That’s an understatement.”

CHAPTER 47

Belgrade, Serbia

Pierce appraised the small mountain of hard drives before him. The sprawling marble entryway of Ethan's house encased him and the FSB officers in silence. Vlad took a step and lifted a rubberized hard drive from the table.

"What's on these?"

Pierce shook his head. "From what I gather, they are all full of videos of global leaders and celebrities having sex with underage victims. Seems to be how this guy operates."

Vlad's face unwound into solemn contemplation. He stared in silence at the pile of media drives on the table. "My men pulled these from the safe. But there was one thing I think you should see."

He walked to the stairs and motioned for Pierce to follow.

The upstairs hallway was lined with watercolor prints of young girls in different positions. Just after a painting featuring a woman pouring a pitcher of milk on her breasts, Vlad turned into an opulent office. A Persian rug spread across a polished hardwood floor. A thick, glass desk positioned in front of a window overlooked the street where the US embassy was located. Dark blue wallpaper bordered dozens of framed photos of Ethan. In each one, his arm casually wrapped around a celebrity, political leader, or head of state.

Vlad glanced back at Pierce. “Our people have been digging. Your CIA has shared much information with us. He circled the desk and simply pointed.

There, on top of a brown leather folio, sat a single white envelope. Pierce read the words on it and his body went rigid.

CHAPTER 48

GeopoliticalTimes.com

BREAKING NEWS

RUSSIA AND USA EMBARK ON AN 'UNPRECEDENTED JOURNEY TO PEACE'

US President John Bright announced only minutes ago that a new deal has been struck between the two superpowers. The world has looked on with confusion and relief as the Naval Harbor in Norfolk, Virginia (USA) welcomed an estimated 100 Russian war ships.

The new peace agreement comes after a week of unverified reports that the Russian fleet has been suffering nuclear radiation leaks and a missing submarine. Online videos of the Coast Guard rescuing Russian sailors have gone viral, some reaching over 30 million views in only the past few hours

CHAPTER 49

Belgrade, Serbia

The black hood around Ethan's head grew more humid by the moment. He'd been tossed into a van and surrounded by the Russians. After a short drive, Ethan's head smacked something hard beside him as the van came to a stop. His finger screamed with pain. It had swollen so much that he could no longer move the hand without blinding agony.

The hood snapped off his head. Light flooded into the van's windows from the streetlights around them. Outside, his lavish mansion stared back at him in sober disappointment. These Russians had no idea what they were doing. They had no idea how the world worked. Very few did, actually.

For seven years, he'd planned this operation with as few people involved as possible. More than a decade ago, he'd heard whispers of an organization of nineteen people called the Order of Safina. While the rich could control the world, *they* manufactured it; they created the reality the rich had the illusion of controlling. Now, his only chance to buy his way into the group was gone.

"Let's go. Inside," one of the men barked.

He staggered sideways to the door, held open by the largest of the men. The man placed a heavy hand on Ethan's shoulder as he stumbled onto his driveway. "Listen to me. We don't want to scare the neighbors. You walk in front of me into the house. If you do anything stupid, I shoot you, put a knife in your hand, and send the names of everyone you've ever known to every terrorist organization on Earth. You get this?"

Ethan nodded. He felt surprisingly numb. Just—nothing. He climbed to his feet and made his way to the front door. The man's hand clenched the fabric of his shirt as they walked.

Inside the foyer, Ethan surveyed the power he'd accumulated over twenty years. The hard drives were by far the most dangerous weapon on earth. Prime ministers, presidents, celebrities, and judges from every country that mattered. They had all done it to themselves. They all had the *choice* not to participate, but they did. Ethan didn't force them to have sex. This was the true nature of power: to aim a flashlight into a very dark corner, forever threatening to turn it on.

"Hey." The large Russian's voice shook him into the moment. "We know you don't have any of these locked with a passkey, but I need you to tell me…is this everything? Is there more somewhere—another place?"

Ethan stared at the pile of hard drives on the marble table, where just this morning he'd placed fresh flowers in a vase.

These fucking morons.

In only a moment, they had destroyed decades of work, the only chance he had at touching the Order of Safina, if it existed at all. All gone. Because these idiots who couldn't comprehend the depth of his power were convinced they were doing the right thing.

"I'll give you two seconds to answer me," the Russian snapped.

"Y-yes. There are copies in the US, but they are all the same. Listen, I've cooperated so far, and—"

"Did I ask you another question?" The Russian's eyes were razorblades.

Ethan's heart pummeled his ribcage. "No. But I—"

"Then don't speak." The man took a step toward him and swept the bag back onto his head. "Lie him on the floor," he barked at the other men.

Calloused hands gripped his torso and arms. Ethan complied as the men lowered him gently to the floor. The stink of the men's sweat was rank, even through the thick burlap bag.

A loud, ripping sound of Velcro echoed around the foyer. Through the tiny holes in the burlap, Ethan watched a man standing over him, pulling off his body armor. He flipped it over his head, and carefully adjusted it. The man then knelt and lifted Ethan's head, sliding the padded, sweaty body armor underneath it.

"We have to keep this clean. Protect the floor," the man said to the others.

The sound of a handgun chambering a round bounced off every surface around him, followed by a pop.

CHAPTER 50

Belgrade, Serbia

Pierce couldn't look away.

"Where did this come from?" he asked.

Vlad lifted his head from a stack of stapled financial documents. "It was in the safe."

Pierce reread the label.

THE ORDER OF SAFINA

He lifted the envelope.

"What is the thing on the label?" Vlad asked, breaking through Pierce's trance.

"Yeah. It's an online conspiracy. Like the Illuminati, but more dangerous. No one actually believes they exist. The internet is full of stupid theories."

Pierce opened the envelope's clasp. A single sheet of paper sat waiting for him. He pulled the page from the envelope and laid it on the desk. Vlad, seemingly unimpressed, continued to rifle through the financial documents.

The page was blank. Just a white sheet of paper.

Why the hell would someone lock up a blank paper?

Pierce held the page up to the lamp on the glass desk and examined it. He didn't really know what he expected to see. A watermark? Indentations? There was nothing. It was probably a long shot, but Pierce withdrew his small Gerber-Recon tactical light and rotated the head to ultraviolet mode.

Even with the lights on in the room, it glowed. On the center of the page, a small symbol of an owl holding a skeleton key. Directly below the owl symbol was a single sentence. Followed by Ethan Peterson's signature, all in ultraviolet ink.

> *I hereby and hereon humbly offer myself for your consideration.*
>
> *Ethan Peterson*

While this wasn't definitive, it would undoubtedly come in handy sometime very soon.

Pierce replaced the paper inside the envelope and stuffed it into his pocket.

Vlad focused on his phone for a moment and lifted his head. "Here it is," Vlad announced. "Right here. Our people in Moscow were right. Ethan has been investing in American military infrastructure and taking out billions in *put-options* on Russian trading companies, betting billions that they would fail soon. If we went to war with your country and our entire fleet fell apart, he would have become a trillionaire within a week. Our intelligence analysts say he would be the richest man in the world."

"That's what all this was. This little shit's bid at tipping the scales. Psychopath." Pierce headed to the door. "I hope he has vodka downstairs."

Pierce exited the room and rounded the upper bannister of the stairs. He stopped, surveying the pile on the table. The most dangerous thing on earth at the moment.

Ethan's lifeless body lay on the floor. A black sack over his head. "You guys going to get rid of him?"

Boris nodded. "We got it. We will use *American* spy technology to get rid of him."

Pierce tilted his head. "American spy technology?"

"Yes," Boris said, smiling. "A pig farm in Northern Belgrade!" He erupted in laughter.

Pierce had worked with Russians in the past. But none who he liked much. He enjoyed this man's approach to the world.

"Good one. Very American of you." Pierce trotted down the stairs. "Kelly is fine. Recovering."

"That's good to hear. What you want to do with all this?" Boris jerked his chin at the table.

"I think some secrets should stay in the dark . . ." Pierce said.

Boris' face twisted in confusion.

". . . but this is not one of them. I'd release the entire thing to the media. I don't care."

"I'm not keeping them. If I give them to Moscow it becomes a weapon. If you turn them in to your government, the same will happen."

"Agreed," Pierce said. "Our local asset here will send them to every media outlet in the world. Exposing the people in the recordings is the only way to remove this weapon's power."

Boris followed Pierce through the foyer into the enormous kitchen. Pierce scanned the room, searching for the bar.

Boris continued as Pierce filled a glass with ice cubes and drenched them in vodka. "Thanks for everything. However, you convinced the admiral to pull the fleet in. You saved a lot of people. Moscow operates as if nationalism and compassion sit on a scale; the higher one is, the lower the other has to be. The only thing they lose is their perspective. We will get this sorted."

Several loud knocks rang throughout the house. Boris shot Pierce a puzzled look.

"It's probably Emir. Our driver. I sent him a text to come pick up all this stuff. He's going to make a few hundred copies and send it out to everyone. The hospital is going to bring Kelly to the private hangar at the airport."

CHAPTER 51

Yorktown, Virginia

Deidra eased back into the leather couch in the HIG living room and stared through the steam wafting from a cup of coffee. She peeled each shoe off as she read the updates from Pierce. The large flatscreen television on the wall was muted. But when Deidra saw a video of Norfolk on the screen, she leaned forward and tapped the volume button on the remote. A helicopter was showing a live aerial view of the harbor. Russian ships filled every pier from end to end.

"... and we are just now receiving word that an anonymous source has obtained video footage of several political leaders engaged in what he described in his email as 'bad behavior.' The footage is set to be released in thirty minutes, and we will be here, as always, to keep you up to date on these bizarre past forty-eight hours we've had.

If the source's claims are true, these videos depict acts that cannot be broadcast to the public. Senator Tim Foster joins us now. Senator, thanks for joining us. We've had an almost surreal day and a half. Can you update us on what's going on in Washington, sir?"

"Sure. Thanks, Linda. We're all grieving the tragic loss of Vice President Braid here in Washington. The President, according to the Twenty-fifth Amendment, is going to need to appoint a new vice president which will be passed through the House. However, those things aren't happening anytime soon. Our sincere prayers go out to the family of Vice President Braid."

"Senator, can you tell us what is happening with Russia at the moment?"

"I'd like to really thank the Joint Chiefs of Staff for developing this Peace Plan and ensuring that peace had a chance to triumph before anything got out of hand. We all came together to ensure the Russians knew we welcomed them with open arms. They've suffered tremendous loss over the past several days, and it's our duty to help them. As I'm fond of saying here in DC, the Cold War is long over. Frankly, I'm immensely proud of the people who—"

Deidra tapped the mute button again. Same old bullshit. Someone does something they disagree with, but when it turns out to benefit society, they gather in a circle to pat each other on the back.

She slid her phone off the coffee table and tapped a message to Pierce.

Thank you. Come on home. See you soon.

CHAPTER 52

GeopoliticalTimes.com

BREAKING NEWS

GLOBAL LEADERS EXPOSED IN MASSIVE LEAK

The US Coast Guard Helicopters are rescuing Russian sailors and American harbors are filled with Russian warships.

As if this couldn't get any stranger, a data leak of videos of heads of state, politicians, and major players engaging in indecent acts with underage people is now online for all to see. The videos have been edited so that the victims aren't identifiable. 97 prominent people have been exposed in the videos so far. We expect many more in the coming hours.

The entire world is about to change.

CHAPTER 53

Belgrade, Serbia

Kelly took a sip from the straw a nurse angled toward her face. One of the doctors, a tall, gangly man with steel-rimmed glasses, ambled into the room with a white plastic bag and laid it on the foot of Kelly's hospital bed.

"We don't have any clothing for you, Miss Kennedy. Some of the nurses have offered a set of scrubs in here I think should fit you. These shoes here should also fit you. The admiral has briefly told us what you have done to save us all. We are all very thankful."

Kelly scooted backward and sat upright. The room spun, but only a little. A wave of nausea bloomed deep within her belly. It painted the room green. The nurse at her bedside snatched a plastic bin from a table. She held it out for Kelly and held Kelly's har back with the other hand. Kelly pitched forward. Her muscles turned to rocks with each dry lurch. Nothing.

She took another sip of water. The doctor came to the IV bag beside her and plunged the contents of a syringe into it. “This is Phenergan. Will help with nausea. I am sending you home with two medicines.” He produced two white plastic bottles from his pocket. “This first one is Phenergan. You can take every four hours as needed to combat the nausea, which may last a few days. This one, however...” The doctor held up the other bottle. “...is just precautionary. The admiral told me someone had been injecting you and he was unsure of the sanitary procedures used. This is an antibiotic called Eritromicin. I think in America they call this Erythromycin. I’ve given you a dose already, so you can take one per day until the bottle is empty. Only for precaution.”

The nausea faded as quickly as it had come. She took the two bottles and placed them on the sheet between her legs. “Thank you.” Kelly’s voice was rough and scratchy, she hadn’t spoken yet. “Sorry. I—”

The doctor raised his hands. “No. Please. It’s fine. You can get dressed in your own time. The admiral is waiting for you. We tell him not to smoke in waiting room, but he is there.”

Kelly nodded and pulled in a breath that stretched her entire chest. The doctor exited through a curtain. The nurse, who apparently spoke little English, motioned to her hand, where the IV was inserted. "I take out. Okay?" Her eyebrows lifted.

Request for approval.

She removed the IV and placed a small bandage on Kelly's hand. The nurse offered Kelly a sympathetic smile, patting her on the shin as she slipped through the curtain.

Kelly peeled open the plastic bag and found a set of neon green scrubs that, surprisingly, were size extra-small. She let her hospital gown crumple to the floor and eyed a bandage in the middle of her chest. While they explained it to her earlier, she hadn't become fully lucid yet. Her eyes drifted down to the still-visible black numbers above her pelvis.

381

She locked out the ensuing thoughts of panic and put on the scrubs. They fit well. She slipped on the old Nike running shoes some sweet nurse somewhere had donated and tied them up. Turning, she examined the room. The clipboard at the foot of her bed read '**НЕПОЗНАТ**' across the top of every document. Kelly took hold of the small stack of yellow and white papers and yanked them from the clipboard, rolled them up, and slid them into the back pocket of the scrubs. Still a little unsteady, she tottered through the curtain into the quiet emergency room.

Aside from a few nurses who tried to look like they didn't notice her, the only sounds were occasional beeps of medical machines chirping unfeeling echoes of the people they were hooked to.

Across the room, in a small waiting area, an older man with short, grey hair stood and faced her. He lowered a cell phone from his ear, tapped the screen, and slipped it into the pocket of his blue jeans. The man strode past the reception desk toward her.

"Miss Kennedy, I'm Dimitri Kostyukov. I helped your friend Pierce Reston with the criminals who took you hostage. I'm glad you made it out all right."

"How long was I out for?"

"I would say it has been a few hours. Mister Reston is coming now. I'm told your plane is waiting. I don't know what agency you are with, but CIA doesn't behave this way. So, please pass along my sincere thanks to your team. You've saved very many—well, potentially millions—of lives here."

Kelly nodded. Still steadying herself. "Thank you. I'm guessing it all worked out. I'm embarrassed I was such a burden. I should have just killed that waste of human flesh before all this happened."

The admiral laughed. “He’s well taken care of now. I can assure you.” He squinted over Kelly’s shoulder. “There’s your partner.”

Kelly beamed. She spun to see Emir’s SUV come to a stop near the front doors. Pierce leapt from the back seat and darted through the doors to Kelly. She wrapped her arms around him.

“You look like shit,” Pierce offered.

Kelly didn’t move her head from his chest. “You smell like shit.”

*****

Pierce was exhausted. He could only imagine how Kelly felt.

As Emir pulled the last of their bags from his vehicle, he arranged them for the flight crew on the slick concrete floor of the private hangar and turned to them with a hand on his chest. “I’m very glad to meet both of you. I hope to see you both again when we aren’t in danger someday.”

The group exchanged goodbyes and Pierce wrapped a jacket over Kelly’s hospital scrubs. As they boarded the plane, the engines crescendoed to a roar.

The pilots welcomed them aboard and the plane taxied out. Kelly pulled a heavy blanket over her body and took a nausea pill. As the aircraft thrust off the runway, Kelly laid her seat back and turned sideways to face Pierce.

"I need a vacation, Pierce. I didn't know the job would be like this," she managed.

Pierce offered a nod. "When we get back, take as much time as you need. Jamaica is gorgeous this time of year."

Within seconds, Kelly was asleep. Pierce tucked a blanket over her feet and poured a glass of vodka from the plane's small freezer.

He dropped back into his seat and flicked on his iPad to a news alert.

GeopoliticalTimes.com

BREAKING NEWS

A WORLD UPSIDE DOWN: PEACE ON THE GROUND - CHAOS AT THE TOP

While we all expected a flood of military conflict rife with political sabre rattling and other nonsense, quite the opposite has occurred.

Russia and the US are now sending each other heart emojis, and global leaders and politicians from every corner of the globe have been publicly exposed in extremely graphic videos with minors. People everywhere are rejoicing in a newfound sense of peace for all, witnessing unprecedented justice for a group of people we all secretly believed to be untouchable. It reminds me of a quote:

"Bad men see good and evil as tools, but so does Karma."

THE END

DRY DEPTH

7.271695072961044S 72.36062752053351E

18.426315N 77.038937W

CONTINUE READING FOR CHAPTER ONE OF THE NEXT BOOK IN THE PIERCE RESTON SERIES,

THE FEAR MAVEN

CHAPTER 1

Miami, Florida

Why the hell does this guy have a gas mask on a plane?

It was most certainly a gas mask. The man beside him in first class had only nudged the duffle bag, but it opened the zipper enough to make out the shape of it in the dark.

Senator Tim Foster had only served five years in office, so his private jet days were still far ahead of him. He regretted taking this flight to Jamaica.

Why would he have a gas mask? It's probably nothing. If I freak out about this, it's going to be all over social media.

As quickly as the plane gained altitude, it angled hard to the left and dove in a steep decline. Tim's stomach lurched into his chest. In the dim light of the cabin, the man beside him slid his duffle bag between his feet and pulled out the black gas mask. Within a second, he'd fastened the black rubber straps behind his head. Tim had no idea what to do. He just stared at the man. Before he could escape his seatbelt, the man beside him produced another black gas mask, then placed in onto Tim's lap. He recoiled at the sight of it.

He fought for breath. The sound of the plane's engines throttled down. They were definitely losing altitude.

"This one's for you," the man offered in a smooth tone. His blue eyes offered no hint of panic.

Tim stared at him in disbelief. "I'm not going to wear this! What the hell is this for? What are you *doing*?"

He tossed the gas mask to the floor and ripped off his seatbelt. As he made to stand, a sharp hiss sizzled behind him. He whipped around. In the cones of light offered by a few reading lamps, Tim watched in horror as a thin, grey fog enveloped the interior of the plane.

Why aren't they freaking out?

"Last chance, Tim."

Tim twisted back to the man beside him, who once again offered him the gas mask. Tim stared, shaking his head. "Who are you? What is this?"

"Listen, Tim. It's coming this way. You only have a few seconds."

Tim eyed the mask, listening for signs of life behind them. Nothing. Were they dead? He snatched the mask and stretched the rubber straps over his head. It sat tight over his face. The sharp smell of rubber filled his nostrils. He sucked panicked breaths through the thick filter.

"Sit down, Tim," the man's muffled voice barked through his mask.

"Fuck you!" Tim tore into the aisle and bounded forward to the galley only two rows ahead. The two female flight attendants who welcomed him onto the plane were strapped into their jump seats. They both withdrew in terror as he rounded the corner with the mask on his face. One of them tore the buckle open on her seatbelt and stood to scream. As she did, her mouth fell open. She collapsed across the lap of the other woman, also unconscious.

Tim knelt and shook her in desperation. Tears trickled down his cheek. The eyepieces of his mask fogged over with his now heaving breaths.

Two giant hands seized him under the arms from behind. In a furious blur, he was slammed back into his seat. A man on either side of him pressed his arms tight against the armrests, using duct tape to secure them.

"Tim, if you don't behave, I'm going to have to knock you out. Understand?" the man shot through his mask.

Tim nodded. What had he done? Were they government?

The man beside him slipped past his knees and into the aisle. Another man joined them, emerging from behind.

One of the men toward the rear of the plane yelled, "Get a few from the back. We're going to need a few pints of blood from at least thirteen passengers. Bring them up here!"

There's more of them?

The cabin lights flicked on. Tim twisted and surveyed his surroundings through the foggy mask lens. The other passengers laid limp in their seats. Their heads lolled to the side, bouncing with the plane's movement. The men wore professional suits. He struggled to breathe through the thick filter of the mask.

"Brian! Pick a few for the crash site. We'll need seat cushion parts, luggage, and a few limbs and teeth. The fatter they are, the more likely their parts are to float to the surface of the ocean, so get those limbs first."

Tim's heart pounded through his temples. Each breath more difficult than the last.

One of the men stood near the unconscious flight attendants in a crisp blue shirt and jacket patted another on the shoulder. "Houdini couldn't have pulled this shit off, boys. We're about to make a whole *plane* disappear."

ACKNOWLEDGMENTS

First, I'd like to thank Michelle (Dizz). She has kept me on track and makes me continue to strive to be a better man.

Second, to my editor/teacher/sensei/coach/ disciplinarian, Deserae Hunter. If you enjoyed this book, she's the reason. She's given me so many critically important lessons in the art of writing. If you need an editor, find her quickly.

@deseraehunter

To my parents, who've set an example of grace and composure throughout my life.

To my sister, who was a home I could escape to no matter where I was on the earth.

ABOUT THE AUTHOR

Chase Hughes is a world-leading behavior expert and served in the US military for 20 years. During his career, he became obsessed with discovering new ways to assist intelligence operations and interrogations. His journey through human potential led him to develop the world's leading courses and techniques for enhanced persuasion and Human Tradecraft™.

From Dr. Phil to hundreds of media outlets, Chase is referred to as the go-to resource for all things persuasion, people-reading, and authority.

Chase retired from the military in 2018 and now trains intelligence agencies, the general public, and businesses in the most advanced human skills. Chase currently resides in Smithfield, Virginia with his family, where he works as an author, keynote speaker, and training provider for the government, and the general public.

Chase Hughes can be contacted through
https://www.chasehughes.com/

@chasehughesofficial

ALSO BY CHASE HUGHES

The Ellipsis Manual
Analysis and Engineering of Human Behavior
(Non-fiction)

The Six-Minute X-Ray
Rapid Behavior Profiling (Non-Fiction)

The Collected Works of Chase Hughes
A Compilation of Articles

Phrase Seven
Pierce Reston Series Book One

A NOTE FROM CHASE:

If you enjoyed the book, please consider leaving a review on Amazon! I read them daily, and they make a tremendous difference to help people discover this series.

★★★★★

I sincerely hope you enjoyed the book, and I hope to see *you* again in book 3!

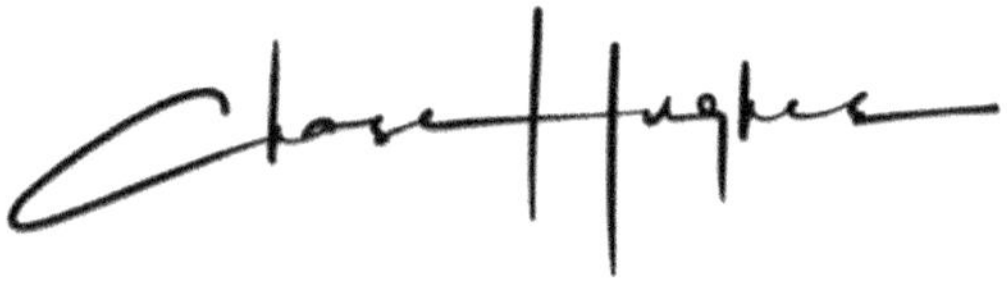

GET THE SKILLS YOURSELF!

Chase Hughes' other books teach HIG skills at an unprecedented level. From behavior profiling to high-end, elite-level influence techniques, Chase's training and material is the global gold standard.

Go to www.chasehughes.com to learn the secrets to advanced persuasion, people-reading, and the art of Human Tradecraft™

A NOTE ON THE FONT

This book is printed in Lexend Deca font to increase reading speed.

In 2000, Bonnie Shaver-Troup theorized there could be a font developed to improve reading speed for regular people and even those with learning disabilities. Lexend was born after years of work.

Lexend has been discussed in two Stanford labs, at HP & Microsoft, was listed on Apple K-12 Assistive Technology from 2003-2005, has recently been referenced in research and patents by Adobe, and is available both on Google Fonts & as an open-source download.

Visit www.Lexend.com to learn more.

WE RISE BY LIFTING
OTHERS

Printed in Great Britain
by Amazon

58184872R00169